CALEN'S CAPTIVE

A SINGULAR OBSESSION BOOK TWO

LUCY LEROUX

PUBLISHED BY: Lucy Leroux
Copyright © 2014, Lucy Leroux
http://www.authorlucyleroux.com
ISBN: 978-1-942336-04-4

First Edition.

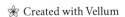 Created with Vellum

DISCLAIMER

This book is a work of fiction. All of the characters, names, and events portrayed in this novel are products of the author's imagination. Any resemblance to actual events or persons, living or dead, is entirely coincidental.

TITLES BY LUCY LEROUX

Making Her His, A Singular Obsession, Book One
Available Now
Confiscating Charlie, A Free Singular Obsession Novelette
Book 1.5
Available Now
Calen's Captive, A Singular Obsession, Book Two
Available Now
Stolen Angel, A Singular Obsession, Book Three
Available Now
The Roman's Woman, A Singular Obsession,
Book Four
Available Now
Save Me, A Singular Obsession Novella, Book 4.5
Coming Soon
Take Me, A Singular Obsession Prequel Novella
Available Now
Trick's Trap, A Singular Obsession,
Book Five
Available Now

Peyton's Price, A Singular Obsession,
Book Six
Available Now

The Hex, A Free Spellbound Regency Short
Available Now
Cursed, A Spellbound Regency Novel
Available Now
Black Widow, A Spellbound Regency Novel, Book Two
Available Now
Haunted, A Spellbound Regency Novel, Book Three
Coming Soon

Codename Romeo, Rogues and Rescuers, Book One
Available Now
The Mercenary Next Door, Rogues and Rescuers, Book Two
Coming Soon

Writing As L.B. Gilbert
Discordia, A Free Elementals Story,
Available Now
Fire: The Elementals Book One
Available Now
Air: The Elementals Book Two
Available Now
Water: The Elementals Book Three
Available Now
Earth: The Elementals Book Four
Available Now

Kin Selection, Shifter's Claim, Book One
Available now
Eat You Up, A Shifter's Claim, Book Two
Available now

Tooth and Nail, A Shifter's Claim, Book Three
Coming Soon

Forsaken, Cursed Angel Collection
Available now

CREDITS

Cover Design: Robin Harper
http://www.wickedbydesigncovers.com

Editor: Rebecca Hamilton
http://qualitybookworks.wordpress.com

Readers: Thank you to all of my guinea pigs! Thanks to Leslie, Kenya, Evelyn, and anyone else I might have forgotten! Special thanks to Jennifer Bergans for her editorial notes. Extra special thanks to my husband for all of his support even though he won't read my sex scenes!

PROLOGUE

he driving beat of the music was starting to make Calen's head pound. He put a weary hand over his eyes, trying to block out the noise and flashing lights of his newest nightclub.

It didn't work.

All he wanted was to go home. He hadn't been here long, but his interest had nosedived after Liam and Trick had left. It used to be the height of his ambition to sit at his own personal VIP table, watching the beautiful people spend their money on his overpriced booze and dance the night away. But the satisfaction of living out this fantasy had faded some time ago.

Liam might be right. Calen needed to find another challenge. Liam wanted him to open a club at the Caislean, the Tyler brothers' flagship hotel here in town. The Caislean chain was starting to open hotels all over the place, but the brothers still took the most pride in their first property. So did he. Calen had helped them find the investors they needed to open their dream hotel, and he was also sentimental about the place. But right now the thought of opening another nightclub held about as much appeal as an all-tofu diet. It did nothing to enhance the arousal he should be feeling, given the determined blowjob he was getting under the table right now.

He was hard enough, he supposed, but nowhere near climaxing. He reached under the long tablecloth, and with a hand on her head, signaled to his lovely companion that she should stop and join him above table. He thanked her politely, and despite her pout, dismissed her as courteously as possible.

Calen had little respect for women who pouted, but in this case, it was helpful. It helped destroy the image he'd first had when he had spotted her. The brunette had been giving him coy and inviting looks all night. For a moment, in the dim light of the club, the fantasy created by her black hair and green eyes had been convincing, so he'd waved her over to keep him company. But she'd only been an illusion —a poor copy of Elynn.

He shifted in his seat uncomfortably. Calen couldn't believe he was still fantasizing about his old university mate's new wife. The fact he'd been doing so regularly since Alex had gotten married was making him crazy. And he felt like total shite about the whole thing.

He waved his manager over and told him to keep an eye on things, then got up to leave. He drove home to his penthouse, still deep in self-flagellation mode. He felt like calling Sergei, if only for the fact that he wasn't the only one of Alex's old friends to find his new bride a little too appealing.

Sergei Damov, Alexandros Hanas, and Giancarlo Morgese had been the first and only friends he had made in University. They had all attended Alex's wedding a few weeks ago at his new Oxford estate and, if circumstances continued as they were, it would be the last wedding among his friends. Giancarlo had technically been married, but the best thing he could say about that disaster is that it had been brief.

With a sigh, he thought back to those early days at University in Edinburgh. It was one of the first times he'd left the country and, miracle of miracles, he'd done it with his father's blessing. No one in the family had ever chosen to study abroad before. In fact, most didn't bother with higher education at all. But he'd known from an early age that he wasn't going to join the family 'business'. He was determined to make his own way in the world, and stay clean doing it.

With his background, he'd had a hard time relating to any of the other people he'd met. Until Sergei. Perhaps friendship between the son of an Irish mobster and the son of a shady Russian magnate was out of the question under normal circumstances, but he and Sergei had felt a connection from day one.

Giancarlo and Alex drifted into their lives shortly after, and soon the four had become inseparable, despite the differences in their personalities. Alex vacillated between being a risk-taker and a control freak. Sergei was like him—easygoing on the outside but with a tendency for too much introspection. Giancarlo had been the steady one, at least on the surface. But still waters ran deep, as they said.

The last time he had seen any of them had been at Alex's wedding. Giancarlo had to leave early after the ceremony, but he and Sergei had stayed on till the bride and groom had shared their last dance. Then he and Sergei had left the reception together to mourn the end of Alex's bachelorhood by getting completely wasted. After drinking half a bottle of vodka, Sergei had admitted how sexy he found Elynn, and Calen had incoherently agreed. They proceeded to try and drunkenly pinpoint exactly why Elynn had affected them the way she had.

In a fog of alcohol-induced intuition, they'd eventually decided it was because of the innocent sensuality she exuded. Between him and Sergei, and before his recent marriage, Alex, the three men had fucked hundreds of beautiful women. Giancarlo's tally had been more modest, but he'd always said it was about quality, not quantity. As for the rest of them, they'd had plenty of models, actresses, socialites, and club girls in their beds. But no other woman of his acquaintance had possessed that look of innocence waiting to be ravaged that Elynn would probably always have. Sergei had mumbled about knowing one other girl with that look, but he'd clammed up when pressed for more details.

Calen had been glad to learn he hadn't been the only one to find his friend's new wife attractive, but it was cold comfort now that he was back home in Boston. In reality, his dissatisfaction with life had begun before he'd attended the wedding, but it had gotten so much worse after he'd returned.

3

He wasn't stupid. He knew he wasn't in love with a woman he'd only met for a few hours. And he had no desire to see her again. He would never hurt his friend by making a pass at his new wife, especially since said wife was obviously completely in love with her husband.

That hadn't stopped him from fantasizing about having what Alex had. He'd even started fantasizing about having kids. But he wasn't about to have one without meeting the right woman first. But those kind of women—one like his friend had now—only came along once in a lifetime, if at all. And they didn't come to men like him. Not to men with families like his.

Arriving at his empty penthouse apartment, Calen started a fire and then took off his suit jacket and tie. Pouring himself a large glass of his favorite whiskey, Knappogue Castle, he collapsed into his newest leather chair and stared broodingly at the fire.

The fireplace was a monster with an austere marble mantelpiece that dominated the large living room. It wasn't one of those modern gas ones. It burned real logs, a smell he loved. The fireplace was the reason he'd bought the apartment in the first place. He spent more nights watching the fire than his 4K OLED flat screen, especially lately when he'd begun to wish he wasn't sitting there alone.

He spent another hour trying to get drunk, but when he couldn't even get a buzz, he gave up and went to bed.

CHAPTER 1

THREE MONTHS LATER...

"What the hell are you talking about? I can't take a meeting for you. You know I don't get involved with your business. Not ever," Calen growled into his phone as he threw on some pants.

It was past noon, but he had still been in bed when his father called. He'd gone to sleep well after dawn, having spent most of the night on his favorite new hobby, photographing fairies. Or rather, looking through security footage for one...

Colman McLachlan sighed deeply on the other end of the line. "Son, I wouldn't be asking you to do this if I had another choice. But your cousin Darren is tied up. His wife broke her leg falling down the stairs. They're worried she might lose the baby, and with all that trouble with little Darren, I can't ask him to do this right now. I'm still at the hospital. They are going to run more tests, and I can't leave them right now. You know how Darren can get. And there's no one else I trust with something this important."

Shit. He wasn't especially fond of Darren's wife, but she was hugely pregnant. A fall at this stage was a serious thing. Still, he had fought hard to maintain his independence from his family, and he wasn't about to jeopardize it.

"Da, I can't meet the Russians. We made a deal. I stay out of your business, and you stay out of mine. I have back-to-back meetings with my distributors all day today."

"You can ask your manager to take those meetings. It's his job. And you won't be doing anything illegal. You're just setting some final terms for the reparations they owe. It won't take more than a half hour of your time."

His father sounded so reasonable, but then he always did. Even at his worst.

Calen swore softly, realizing he had no choice. About a month ago, a small Russian crew under the Komarov umbrella had made the mistake of setting up an enterprise in a neighborhood run by the McLachlan family. They had taken initiative, not bothering to check with their superiors when they built a large meth lab on the ground floor of an apartment complex that was part of the McLachlan's legitimate holdings. A few distant cousins had lived in the building, on the second floor. The fumes had poisoned their little girl. She didn't make it.

Calen had felt the same rage over her death that his father and cousins did, even if he hadn't known her. She had been four years old, still a baby. The Russians had discovered exactly how badly they had fucked themselves shortly afterwards. He didn't know how many had ended up dead at his family's hands. The chemist and his boss for sure, right after the incident. He didn't want to know if any others had followed. The Russians had decided against a full-blown war and had offered reparations instead.

Apparently, he was about to find out exactly what those reparations were.

Maia's heart felt like it was going to explode out of her chest. She was running flat out, her energy reserves long gone. There was a stitch in her side and another under her breast that was making it hard to catch her breath, but she couldn't stop. If they caught her, she was dead.

Pumping her already trembling legs harder, she scrambled down a ridge and across a muddy pit, praying that she had lost her pursuers.

She had thought she'd gotten so lucky today. Her boss had asked her to do him a favor. He was teaching an introductory Entomology class and he'd wanted live specimens for a demonstration. Maia had to check her traps for the moths she studied so she hadn't minded making the trek out to the woods. She had found an assortment of beetles and walking sticks. Then she had seen a rare species of butterfly, a Long Tailed Skipper, flying overhead.

That species wasn't normally found so far up north. Maia had been eager to take a picture of it so she could add it to the butterfly count. Her lab kept logs on the numbers of butterflies spotted each season in order to determine population numbers.

The dusky blue and grey butterfly had flown just out of the range of her camera lens. She'd doggedly pursued it, crashing through bushes and over fallen logs and uneven terrain. Her lab's record keeping was strict. You had to take a time-stamped picture in order to add the specimen to the count.

The Skipper continued to elude her, flying over a ridge. Panting slightly, she climbed up the steep incline until she topped the rise and found herself at the edge of a small ravine. All thoughts of the butterfly promptly fled, even as it flew past the heads of the men at the bottom of the ridge.

Two men, one in a baseball cap and the other bareheaded, were dropping a partially covered body into a hole near the bottom on the ridge. Coming up above them, she had stopped short in shock, the air leaving her lungs. She'd been so stunned, she'd simply frozen like an idiot directly in front of them.

Both men had seen her almost right away. And she had seen them clearly, too. Neither was disguised. They weren't wearing masks. The taller, more muscled one, was covered in tattoos. His shorter and fatter partner, the one closest to her, had some as well, but they were fewer. The fat man's beady dark eyes had narrowed when they met hers. The giant behind him had shouted, and the heavier one had lunged for her. But he'd been too far away, and she'd dropped everything to run as fast as her legs could carry her.

At first, she thought she was going to get away. She was small, but fast—faster than the heavy man pursuing her. In junior high, she had set the record in the four-hundred-meter dash. Behind her, the fat man had chased her, and she'd quickly gotten ahead of him. But she wasn't fast enough to escape his larger and fitter partner.

There were crashing noises behind her, but Maia's heart was pounding almost hard enough to drown them out. All she knew was that she had to keep running. She was flying over the uneven terrain when she tripped the first time and went down hard. The knees of her jeans tore, and she could feel that telltale painful friction that told her she'd scraped herself bad enough to bleed. Ignoring the pain, she struggled to her feet and kept running up the hill near her car.

Suddenly, a large hand grabbed her, its weight enough to send her crashing to the ground once more. Then he was on top of her. The giant grabbed her by the calf, dragging her toward him. She thought she was too out of breath to scream, but she managed to do it anyway. Her attacker flipped her over violently, grabbing her by the legs and waist. She screamed again and kicked out as hard as she could. One of her kicks landed against his stomach, but the giant only grunted before hauling her close enough to backhand her with brutal strength.

Pain exploded across the left side of Maia's face, and she crumpled to the ground like a broken marionette. The ground rose up to meet her, but she barely felt its impact. Inhaling dirt, her vision went momentarily black. Rough hands hauled her up, and she was swinging over the ground, back in the direction of the rough grave.

She turned her eyes to the man carrying her. He looked down at her without expression, his dark eyes flat and cold. The world swam, and the trees became a swirl of green and grey. One blow, and she was done fighting. The most she could hope for was to stay conscious.

"Please," she whispered to her attacker through sore and rapidly swelling lips.

He ignored her as they came upon the fat man. She could still make him out despite the darkness encroaching on her vision. He was sweaty and out of breath. Bent nearly double, he rested his hands on his thighs before shooting her a look of hatred. But there was another emotion in his eyes as well.

Lust.

THE BLINDFOLD SMELLED of oil and gasoline. Maia's hands were tied behind her, looped to the rope binding her ankles together. Terrified, she cried silently. She had tried screaming when they had stuffed her in the van, hoping someone would hear her. But the blow that followed had taught her to keep quiet. And now she couldn't hear any traffic noises close enough to make screaming worth it. Not that she could scream with the disgusting rag in her mouth.

Maia wasn't sure why she wasn't already dead. She had thought she was about to join the other body in the shallow grave out in the woods. But it wasn't going to be that easy. No, she was pretty sure she was going to suffer horribly before she died. The way that porky little man had looked at her filled her with dread.

Squeezing her eyes shut, she tried to calm down enough to think of a plan—any plan to save herself.

CHAPTER 2

*C*alen was fucking pissed. He still couldn't believe he was doing this. He had rearranged his meetings and called in Mike, his head of security at the club, in addition to Jay, his regular driver and bodyguard, to go with him to the meet. That had been before Jimmy O'Donnell had showed up, courtesy of his father. The older man had been his own bodyguard growing up. Now he was high up in his father's organization. The old man trusted him implicitly. Taking Jimmy along made a lot of sense, but Calen resented it. He hated the whole fucking situation.

And apparently this fucking meeting is in the goddamned middle of nowhere.

Dilapidated warehouses filled the skyline as his town car wound down one narrow alleyway after another. He hated the closed-in feeling the crowded buildings gave him. But he was careful not to let that show on his face. He had learned to control his facial expressions and body language a long time ago. Besides, it wouldn't do to let Jimmy see he was rattled. He liked him, but Jimmy was loyal to Colman, not him. And Calen never let his father see him sweat, not even vicariously. Pissed yeah. But never rattled or nervous. It was one of the only lessons he'd learned from his father that he actually found useful.

"You'll be fine. You're a scarier-looking motherfucker than your old man." Jimmy nodded approvingly from seat across from him. "Just make sure they don't lowball you on the settlement. The more you get, the more little Mary's parents get. They'll want to have more kids someday."

Calen idly wondered how much of a cut his dad was going to take, but decided not to make an issue out of it. And personally, he found his father's rounder and jovial-looking face incongruously intimidating. Much more so than the harder angular planes of his features, inherited from his mother's side of the family. By comparison, Colman looked harmless, but appearances were deceiving. It was like getting close to a friendly rabbit—when it turned on you and savaged your arm, it was always a complete surprise.

Not that it mattered. He was here. Not his father. "Don't worry. I know how to play hardball," he muttered, still staring out the window.

If he hadn't learned how to negotiate, he wouldn't own a dozen nightclubs right now. All clean operations. Mostly. Here and there he may have made a deal in the shady grey area, but for a man in his business, that was sometimes necessary. But Calen was satisfied he'd always colored inside the lines.

They finally pulled in front of the right warehouse. Gesturing to Jay to wait outside with the car, he and Jimmy made for the door with Mike at their heels. His security chief walked ahead of him, busily scanning the area for potential threats. Some habits were hard to break when you had spent a decade in the military and almost as long as a mercenary.

Mike had spent half his life in some of the most hellish places on earth and Calen had jumped at the chance to hire him. Though Mike worked at Siren at the moment, his newest club, he was in charge of security at all of them. He preferred to move between them as needed, so Calen was glad he was still in town until Siren was better established.

Following Mike's lead, Calen stepped into the dimly lit interior of the warehouse. Smaller rooms branched off a larger central open space. Next to him, a set of metal stairs led to a walkway that was also surrounded by smaller rooms. Another set of stairs at the back led to the walkway and a windowed supervisor's office that overlooked the whole room.

It was dusty. Calen could smell mold and the bleach that was presumably used to treat it. Scanning the room, his eyes took in a mostly empty space. At the far end, four men argued in Russian.

His grasp of the language wasn't as good as when he and Sergei lived together, but it was passable. Two men were berating a larger muscled man while a third fatter one stood there, seemingly uncon-cerned with the shouting. Calen paused in the shadows by the door, gesturing to the others to stay quiet.

"I'm going to the toilet. Bring her inside," the fat one ordered as he walked away to a staircase leading to a suite of offices visible on the right.

"What the fuck is this, Viktor?" one man in a suit spat out as the fatter man disappeared.

The muscled man shrugged. "Timur wants to play with her a bit before he kills her."

Timur. Calen recognized the name.

The other man sighed while the first one continued. "How much did she see?"

"Enough," Viktor replied.

"Will she be missed?"

Viktor shrugged again. "Probably. She has a Harvard student ID."

Calen's ears perked up. What the hell was going on? Why did they have a Harvard student? If one went missing, it would make the news. Why take the chance?

"Is she worth anything?"

"Doesn't look like she has money. Maybe to the right buyer, but Timur won't take the chance of letting her live."

The other man nodded, and a fifth man came down from the office. He and Viktor went out a door near them. It presumably led outside because he heard a door slam and then Viktor came in carrying a small bound girl over his shoulder in a fireman's hold. He pulled her off him to display her to the other men.

A thrill of recognition passed through Calen as he got a better look at the petite frame and orange-gold hair of the prisoner.

She was too far away to be sure, but he was almost convinced he'd found his fairy.

***

THE CRYING girl had been shoved out of sight into a side room as soon as he stepped out into the brighter light in the center of the warehouse. He walked confidently to the men, emotionless mask intact.

"Gentlemen. I am Calen McLachlan. I believe you are expecting me," he said coldly.

"Yes, please sit down," the man in the suit said. "I am Peter. I represent the Komarov family."

"Why isn't Timur Komarov representing the family?" he asked flatly.

The men shifted in surprise, eyeing each other across the table.

"I speak for the family. Timur is...busy," Peter said cautiously.

Calen took a seat and sat down in a deceptively relaxed pose. "Tell him to finish fuckin' pissing himself and get out here."

Peter and the others looked at each other again. Apparently the Komarov heir didn't do business much. Whether or not it was because he wasn't trusted remained to be seen.

Calen could tell that they didn't want to agree. Even Mike was probably wondering what the fuck he was doing. He could feel Jimmy's eyes boring a hole into the back of his head, but he knew the old man wouldn't give any sign he thought Calen's request odd. Jimmy had also taken a few lessons from his old man.

He crossed his arms and waited. He wanted Timur here, with him. As long as he was in sight, the fat fuck wasn't in the side room putting his greasy hands on his fairy.

***

Timur was a pompous stupid bastard. He didn't live up to his father's cutthroat reputation. Neither did Calen, but unlike the piece of shit in front of him, he wasn't living like a blood-sucking tick off his father's largess. The man stank of sweat and lust.

For the most part, Timur was paying attention, but periodically his eyes would shift to the side room where the girl was, like he simply couldn't help himself. But it was to Calen's advantage to have the enemy in front of him for assessment. And what he saw was mostly weakness and greed.

Peter was easier to deal with. He was a straight shooter that had been ordered to satisfy his demands...within reason. The McLachlans were older and more established in Boston. His father kept more neighborhoods in his iron grip than the Russians, and the docks were his. The Russians moved shit only with his father's grace. Calen was in a stronger position, and Peter knew it.

"One hundred," Peter said after twenty minutes of downright nasty negotiations.

"My price is two," Calen replied, inflexible.

Peter shifted, betraying his discomfort while his men whispered in the background. The Komarov had probably set a fixed ceiling somewhere in between one and two hundred grand.

Calen went in for the kill, switching to Russian, "But I will settle for one fifty and the girl."

"What girl?"

"The one you just brought in. I want her."

The Russians fell silent. Then Timur started shouting bloody murder. The men behind him shifted nervously. Jimmy moved closer to Calen's back while Mike flanked the Russians, keeping the larger Viktor in front of him.

Peter's professionalism shone brightly. He, like Calen, didn't move. He switched to Russian as well. "Your grasp of our tongue is very good. You honor us with your skill."

"Thank you, but flattery won't change my mind. I want the girl," Calen continued in Russian.

"I'm afraid that's not possible," Peter said, glancing sideways at Timur, who had quieted down after his initial outburst.

Not as stupid as he looks, Calen thought, shooting Timur a look before shifting his attention back to Peter.

"Then we're done here. There is no deal. There is no more looking the other way at the docks, either," he bluffed.

He didn't have the ability to make that call, but the man in front of him didn't know that. Standing, he turned, noting with satisfaction that both Jimmy and Mike were stone-faced, backing his play even if they didn't understand what was going on. He ignored the hissed argument between Timur and Peter.

"Two hundred it is," Peter called after him.

Calen turned around. "Now it's two hundred *and* the girl."

"I'm afraid that's not possible. Our guest is unable to...leave us," Peter said in an apologetic tone.

Calen smiled and walked back to the table. He leaned over it and braced his hands on the surface. "Your people cost me family. Now I expect you to reimburse me. I'll be taking the girl with me. I can assure you, I will keep her close. She won't be a problem. Why don't you bring her out here."

Peter and Timur began to argue again, but Calen waved them into silence.

"I give you my personal assurance—and my father's—that you will not hear from her again. Whatever your reason for extending your hospitality to..." he paused and gestured to Viktor.

"Maia," the muscled man eventually growled, crossing his arms.

"Yes. Whatever your reason for keeping Maia here, it's now moot. She will belong to me and my family. You won't hear from her again. Now bring her out here."

It took a lot more arguing, but Calen refused to budge. Eventually Peter nodded in resignation, and Viktor was sent to get the girl. Timur was nearly apoplectic, but Calen didn't care. He'd won. Two hundred grand for Mary's parents and Maia for himself.

He stepped back, his body tensing slightly as the girl was brought out. She was wearing jeans and a black puffy coat that was dirty and torn. She was still gagged, and her hands were still tied in front of her, but her feet were unbound. Calen walked closer to her as she stared at everyone with wide eyes, trembling in the larger man's grasp.

His insides twisted as he saw her more closely. It really looked like her. His fairy. The one he'd spotted that night in his club.

Only once in real life had he caught a glimpse of the girl he now referred to as his fairy; she'd been walking past him in the hallway at Siren a few weeks ago. She had looked so out of place. She was small, with curves proportional to her frame, and that night she'd been wearing a loose, knee-length dress. Every other girl in the place had on something skintight and short enough to make a whore blush. But not her.

Her hair was such a strange shade—gold and orange. It had caught his eye right away, and when he lost her in the crowd, he'd looked for her in the club's security footage for the night.

She'd only been in the frame for a minute, in the midst of a group of girls the cameras had caught better. But he'd seen enough. It had been her discomfort with the scene around her that had cemented his interest. That and her sweet fey looks. She looked like a wood nymph, or a Christmas elf.

Now here she was, still beautiful in a strange, unconventional way. Her fragile-looking nose was completely red from crying. Her features were dainty, with a little chin that was a tiny bit pointed and these huge eyes. Except right now she wouldn't look at him, as if she had suddenly realized that looking at them directly would make her chances of survival worse.

Calen couldn't stop himself from reaching out to touch her. She flinched as he touched her small cheek, but he didn't stop.

"Hello, Doll," he said quietly in English, trying to comfort her with his steady, even tone.

Startled, she looked at him for the first time. He was careful to show no reaction as he saw her eyes. They were remarkable, a blue-green close to teal. At least what he could see of them. One of them was swelling shut. He lowered his head.

"It's going to be all right," he whispered in her ear. "Take my property out to the car," he said more loudly, gesturing to Mike.

The girl's eyes flared in fear and surprise, and she whimpered slightly. Her eyes went glassy as Mike took her by the shoulders.

"That bitch won't be worth jack shit on the street. She won't earn piss," Timur hissed in Russian. "Too skinny and ugly. No one will pay to fuck her," he continued, not acknowledging the fact that he'd clearly been planning on fucking her himself—while he cut her to pieces, if Calen remembered his reputation correctly.

He didn't answer as Mike guided Maia out of the warehouse. "I'm not planning on selling her," he eventually replied in English. "I have other plans for her."

CHAPTER 3

*M*aia didn't know what to do. She thought about running, but the large man who looked like a boxer had her firmly by the shoulder. He'd tried to put her in the car, but she'd struggled until he'd stopped trying. He scanned the area for something—cameras, maybe—and propped her against the car.

After a moment, the other two men came out. The younger, nicely dressed one came up to her and removed her gag. He was tall with chestnut brown hair and icy blue eyes. Heart pounding, she waited for him to say something, but he simply stared down into her face. Running wouldn't help now. She wouldn't get far if she tried. He reached for her, and she flinched involuntarily, but he just went for her wrists. He untied the rope that bound them, then rubbed the red marks the rope had left gently with his thumbs.

"My name is Calen McLachlan, and you belong to me now," he said, his pale blue eyes boring into hers.

Unable to stop shivering, she looked up at him. "W—W—What does that mean?" she stuttered.

She never stuttered, but she was terrified.

"It means you come with me. You live with me. You do what I say, and you stay alive. Or you stay here and die," he said, opening the car door for her and waiting outside of it.

Fear coursed through her veins like mercury. Freezing cold, her gaze darted all around, and her breath came out in pants. Calen looked over her head to exchange a look with one of the guards before extending his hand, but she shrank away from it.

"You have to calm down. I'm not going to hurt you. And I'm not going to let anyone else hurt you. But you can't stay here. You have to come with me now, or I won't be able to do anything for you. Get in the car. Please," he added, still holding his hand out to her.

Maia gulped down air, trying to slow her breathing. She looked at the door of the warehouse and back to the open car door. What choice did she have?

She wobbled on unsteady legs. Calen's hand was still outstretched, but she didn't take it, making her way to the car door in a slow, painful walk. She hesitated there, meeting Calen's eyes in humiliation and shame.

"I can't sit there. I..." she trailed off and looked away, embarrassed.

Calen's eyebrows sank into a deep V, but then his eyes widened as if in realization. There was the faintest trace of urine in the air. She was mortified, but she hadn't been able to help it. She had been tied up for hours.

Calen pulled off his leather coat. "It's okay. You can wear this."
She hesitated.

"Seriously," he said. "It's okay. I have four or five of them."
How many?

She gave him a funny look, but took the coat and wrapped it around herself. It fell well below her knees. Stepping into the car gingerly, she slid into the seat, favoring her right side. Calen followed her and the older guard climbed in after him while the one that looked like a boxer joined the driver in the front. Maia curled into the corner of the car opposite the men, trying to make herself as small as possible.

"What's your name?" Calen asked. "Your full name."
Maia licked her lips nervously. "Maia Elizabeth Dahl."

"*Doll?* Your name is actually doll?"

"It's D-A-H-L, but that's why I thought you knew me. It sounds like doll," she whispered.

"And you go to Harvard? What do you study?"

She looked at him nervously. How did he know that? Oh yeah, her wallet.

"Entomology. I'm a graduate student." After a moment, she continued, "They kept my ID. My wallet."

"All of your belongings, including your car, will be delivered to my people within the hour. We'll have them moved to my place for you later."

Maia watched him gravely. Was he serious? "Are you actually taking me home with you?"

"It's the safest place for you right now."

He switched to another language to address the older guard. *Was he speaking Gaelic?*

Maia sank into the seat and watched the two men interact. Whoever this younger man was, he was powerful. The older one was tough-looking with silver hair and an air of quiet menace, yet he deferred to Calen like he was talking to a young Michael Corleone.

What the hell have I gotten myself into?

"INFORM my father about my new houseguest and make sure the Russians return all of her things. I want them swept for bugs and toxins," Calen told Jimmy as he watched Maia studiously avoid looking at them.

"Toxins? You think they'd cross you by poisoning her?" Jimmy replied in the same language.

His father insisted all of his top lieutenants and family spoke the mother tongue.

"I don't know, but I don't trust them. Timur is a crazy piece of shit. He might be stupid enough to take this personally."

"Are you going to ask her why they had her in the first place?"

"Later. She's in shock, and she needs a doctor. Some of the bones in her face may be fractured, judging by the swelling."

Jimmy glanced at Maia. "Are you seriously going to keep her with you?"

Calen looked at Maia, too. She was huddled in his coat, probing at her swollen cheek with a shaky hand. But she wasn't crying, and the trembling had eased to an occasional shudder. She was trying so hard to be strong. He had to admire that.

"If I have to."

"If you want to keep her alive, you probably do."

MAIA STARED at the parking garage around her. Calen was giving orders to his men, and the older one appeared to be leaving after a bit more conversation in Gaelic. At least she *thought* it was Gaelic. Her mother hadn't spoken it, although she'd been half Irish. But her mother had been born in Florida, not Ireland, and she'd never had much interest in her heritage.

She tried not to look as freaked out as she felt when Calen finished his conversation and gestured for her to join him and the other two men at the elevator. Calen pressed his thumb to a glossy black pad, and the doors closed. They rode in silence, and Maia wondered where the hell she was. She'd only ever seen thumb print locks on television.

The elevator ride seemed much longer than it probably was. Holding her breath, she looked at Calen out of the corner of her eye. *Please don't let him be an axe murderer. Or worse.*

The elevator doors opened directly onto the top floor penthouse, and Maia exhaled with a little whoosh. Beyond a small foyer, there was a bar on the left. It was stocked with gleaming glass bottles that caught the light. Across from it was a doorway. Beyond it to the right there was a spacious living room with a breathtaking view of the city. A massive fireplace dominated the space, which was filled with comfortable-looking leather furniture.

"I'll show you to your room. I'm sending for a doctor. He should be here soon. You may want to shower while I find you some clothes," Calen said when she didn't move from the entrance. "I can show you around later."

Filled with panic, she whirled to face him. "Do I really have to stay here?" she whispered.

His eyes flared with something that might have been sympathy. "I'm afraid so. For a while, at least."

Maia stared at him. "How long is a while?"

He raked his hand through his hair and shrugged, looking tired.

"Days? Weeks? Months?" she asked.

Calen stood a little straighter but didn't respond.

"Years?" she whispered.

He shifted his weight. "If it comes to that, we'll find a solution that works...for both of us. Why don't you shower?"

Maia followed him numbly, limping to a bright room done in grey and navy. It was a million times nicer than her shabby little studio apartment with its warped floors and windowsill that let in the cold during winter. Everything here was expensive and luxurious. Even if the impersonal decor made it seem more like a hotel room than where someone lived.

Calen showed her where the bathroom was and then left to find her something to wear. Maia stepped into the bathroom, which was well stocked with soaps and shampoos and fluffy navy blue towels. She shrugged Calen's leather coat off, hoping like crazy she hadn't gotten any urine on it. She had peed herself a little in the woods, during the attack. She'd been so embarrassed when he'd given his coat to her. But there hadn't been any ridicule or pity in his eyes.

You belong to me now.

Had he been serious? Was he going to sell her? She didn't think she would make much money as a prostitute, but she did look young. She still got carded for R-rated movies. There were a lot of sickos out there who wanted the illusion of a young girl. But Calen hadn't sounded like he meant to do her harm. If he was going to prostitute her, why bring her back here? This was obviously his home.

If she was going to find out what he actually wanted, she needed to shower and get back out there.

Maia washed carefully. Her face stung, but she didn't think anything was broken. Hopefully. She knew her eye was swelling but not too badly. The view in the mirror had shown her as much. Purple and green bruises dotted the left side of her face. When she took off her clothes more were visible on her body, many in the shape of fingerprints. As the adrenaline wore off, her ankle throbbed more and more. She must have sprained it in the woods, but she hadn't even felt it until the warehouse.

Once she was done, she wrapped herself in a fluffy towel, not wanting to touch her soiled clothes again. She industriously began to wash them in the sink with shampoo and hung them to dry on the shower door. When she walked back into the bedroom, she limped to a stop. Calen was waiting for her, holding a pile of clothes in his hands.

"I don't have anything that will fit you, but I brought you some of my belts so you can adjust some of this stuff. I called a doctor. He's on his way. And you may want to wait to get dressed until the exam is done so I brought you a robe in the meantime. You should probably stay off that foot till the doctor takes a look at it. Are you hungry?"

Maia nodded, the move small and tentative.

"Why don't we start with soup?" he asked, his hands out and open.

Soup?

As if on cue, her stomach rumbled loudly. Nodding miserably, she clutched the towel closer. He gave her a reassuring little smile and left the room. Slipping off the towel, she pulled on the robe. It must have been Calen's because it was ridiculously large on her. Fingering the soft terry cloth, she climbed onto the bed, hugging a pillow tightly as she waited.

CHAPTER 4

Calen moved to his kitchen and rummaged through his shelves for soup. Would Maia prefer clam chowder or cream of mushroom? Or something with beef?

Jay and Mike wandered into the kitchen. "Jimmy called," Jay said. "Your father has been informed of the results of your negotiations. He expressed some concern."

"I got what he wanted, and I got what I wanted. He needn't concern himself with the details," Calen said with a frown, pouring a can of clam chowder into a saucepan.

The two men shifted their weight and gave each other meaningful looks, but he didn't care. He knew they didn't disapprove, exactly. Both of them were good guys, and they would have done the same thing in his place. No, their concern was about what might happen next—what the Russians might do if they suspected he might let Maia go free. Sighing, he dug through a drawer for a spoon to stir the pot.

"Is she the one you've been looking for, boss?" Mike asked.

Calen met his eyes then. *Of course*. Mike had delivered the security footage to him on occasion, before they started sending a feed from the club directly to this penthouse. His security chief had been in his office the night he'd started looking for his fairy, staying late in case she showed up in person. A still of her had been on a monitor for comparison.

"I'm not sure," he finally answered. "Looks like her though."

"Yeah, she does," Mike said while Jay frowned in confusion.

"You saw the girl before?" Jay asked curiously. "Where?"

"At the club."

Jay frowned in confusion. "Why were you looking for her?"

Calen shrugged. "I'm not sure. She just...she didn't look real."

And it was true, Calen reflected later as he watched the doctor examine Maia from the door to her room. Up close, she looked like his childhood fantasy of an elf or fairy. Her hair and those eyes, the delicate features that were just a little pointed.

Her skin, the part that wasn't bruised, seemed to glow with a pearlescent luster that wasn't normal without cosmetics. He was pretty sure she was the girl he'd spotted in his club, but confirmation of that would have to wait until after the exam.

Maia finished her soup as the doctor arrived. When they were laying out their equipment, he'd insisted on a full set of X-rays. Calen suspected several of her delicate bones might be fractured or broken.

The doctor was part of a larger concierge service he used at a few of his east coast clubs. But this particular doctor owed him a favor. Eric Tam was originally from Vegas, where he'd developed a gambling problem. Calen had been doing an on-sight inspection at his club on the strip that day. Tam had been brought to his attention when he couldn't pay his bill. Calen forgave the debt in exchange for work in trade. When the doctor proved useful, Calen pushed him into Gambler's Anonymous. A few months later he'd recommended him to the company he now worked for.

Eric had been led to believe a VIP had gotten out of control with a waitress. It was understood that a police report wouldn't be filed for the attack. Calen could tell the doctor didn't like it, though.

"Maia, I want to reassure you that this is a safe place," Eric said in his reassuring doctor tone as his PA cleaned the scrape on Maia's knee.

Wide-eyed Maia nodded and Eric leaned in. "Do you need a sexual assault exam?" he asked softly.

At the door, Calen tensed. He hadn't thought about the time before the warehouse, of her actual capture. He had assumed Timur hadn't had time, but now he wasn't sure.

"No," Maia said, wincing from the sting of the antiseptic.

Eric looked over his shoulder at Calen before turning back to the nymph on the bed. "Would you like your boss to leave?" Eric asked quietly.

Calen didn't like the idea of that at all, but he said nothing.

"No, really. I don't need one. I didn't lose consciousness at all. I was dazed, but I stayed awake, and I don't need one," Maia whispered. "I was too terrified to let myself pass out."

Calen didn't want to think about what might have happened to Maia if she had lost consciousness. He crossed his arms, fantasizing about punching Timur in the face, but he was careful not to let his anger show. It might scare Maia.

"Okay, that's good," Eric said reassuringly, applying a bandage to her face where the skin had split high on her cheekbone.

He'd already put a splint on her hand where she had two sprained fingers. Her ankle was also sprained, but thankfully not broken. He told Calen to leave then, announcing that he needed to wrap her ribs because two were cracked.

Calen went back out to the kitchen to wait. He'd asked Mike to cook the beef wellington his housekeeper had left prepared in the fridge along with some potatoes. It was almost ready. Mike was going to stay on for dinner so they could discuss security. He wanted more men to watch his place, and wherever Maia went from now on.

"I'm calling in some men I used to serve with. They are in the private sector now. At least two are free to start immediately. They're good, solid," Mike said after making a few calls. "How many are you going to want?"

"Better double that. They can start Monday. I have a meeting then, and she's going to want to go back to school eventually. I want to be able to have them work in shifts. One of them should double as a driver, too. She goes nowhere alone."

"Understood," Mike said while helping to set the table. "I can set up some other safeguards here. We'll have to surveil her work."

"Yeah, do that," Calen replied as the doctor emerged from Maia's room.

"She might have a problem with that," Mike added.

"Do it anyway," he ordered as he went to meet Eric halfway.

He sat in the living room while the PA began to pack their medical gear.

"She has a hairline fracture in her hand and a few cracked ribs," the doctor began. "The sprain in her ankle is going to cause a few problems, too. She doesn't need to be hospitalized, but she should rest for the next few days. I'll leave a set of crutches. She should stay off that ankle for a while. Does her place have an elevator?"

"She'll be staying here until she's better," Calen said evenly, not offering the possibility that the situation might be long-term.

Eric's head drew back in surprise. The doctor had done a lot of work for Calen in the past at his clubs, here and in Vegas. He'd patched up people injured in brawls, treated ODs and alcohol poisonings. In every incident, Calen had been detached, more annoyed at the interruption to his business than anything else.

Calen hated the weakness in people that allowed them to get in those situations, although he'd always been sympathetic when a woman had been involved. Up to a point. Keeping one here, in his home, was out of character, but he didn't care what the doctor thought as long as he did his job.

"Okay, well, call me if there is any change," Eric said, and he and his assistant left.

MAIA WAS TESTING out her new crutches when Calen came to get her for dinner. She was wearing one of his larger sweaters as a dress, using a belt to make it fit. A pair of his thick winter socks covered her feet. Apparently she wasn't moving fast enough for him because he came and took her crutches away.

"Hold on," he said, and before she could protest, he swung her into his arms.

He carefully avoided the wrap around her ribs with one arm above it and another under her knees.

"You don't have to carry me," she said nervously. "I need to get used to the crutches."

"Let the swelling go down more. Don't worry, the dining room isn't far," he replied. "Mike is joining us for dinner. He's my head of security."

Heat rushing to her cheeks, Maia tried to shrink into herself as Calen carried her down the hallway, past the living room and into another hallway. The penthouse was the largest apartment she had ever seen. It was bigger than any house she'd ever been in.

Calen pushed open a door, and they entered a formal dining room. Like the guest bedroom, it was elegant and austere, with a long dark wooden table and chairs. Everything looked clean and modern, but a little too cold for her personal tastes.

As if those matter, she thought silently. What she liked and what she wanted no longer mattered.

You belong to me now.

She peeked at Calen from under her lashes. What did he want from her? Why had he saved her? She wasn't sure if he meant it when he'd said he wouldn't hurt her. A worse fate might be waiting for her. That thought made her tense, a move that hurt her ribs. She exhaled slowly, willing her body to relax.

"Do you need another pain killer?" Calen asked with concern. "The doctor left you a bottle."

"I'm okay," Maia said, fingering the tablecloth.

It was a heavy silk damask, which would probably be ruined if she spilled something. Suddenly paranoid about making a mess, she glanced over at the other man, Mike, the one that resembled a heavy-weight boxer.

He was massive, almost as large as the Russian in the woods. He had tattoos on his arms, but these weren't in Cyrillic. They looked military. When he looked over at her, his eyes were kind, and she relaxed a bit more.

"Is there anyone waiting for you?" Mike asked.

"No, it's just me. Me and work people. My mom died a few years ago. I live alone," she said.

Her voice sounded a little weak to her own ears.

"No boyfriend?" Mike asked, giving Calen a surreptitious glance she didn't understand as he poured her a glass of water.

Calen and Mike were drinking wine, but Calen apologetically told her she couldn't have any with her pain medication.

"No," she replied, taking her glass awkwardly.

The fingers on her right hand were sprained so she couldn't use it well. But using her left was worse. In the end, she used both hands. Looking up, she saw Calen watching her attentively.

"Girlfriend?" Mike continued questioning her.

Maia's lips twitched. "*No. What do you secure?*" she asked him.

"I'm in charge of security for all of Mr. McLachlan's nightclubs. I'm based at Siren right now."

She looked directly at Calen. "You own Siren? I've been there. Once..."

"Really? When?" he asked.

"Um, like three weeks ago. It was a Friday," she said, meeting his eyes in silent appraisal.

Would a successful club owner also be a pimp? As if reading her mind, Calen gave her a huge smile. It was probably meant to be disarming, but she found it intimidating. He had a lot of straight white teeth— like a very handsome shark.

He continued to smile at her expectantly.

"It's a nice club," Maia said when he didn't say anything.

"Thanks," he said, then took a sip of wine. "Did you have fun?"

She nodded. "Yes, although we didn't stay long." He waited, and eventually she filled in the rest. "It was for a friend's birthday. I'm not sure how she got us in, but she didn't want to stay."

"Why not?" Mike asked.

Maia frowned. "She thought she saw her cousin and wanted to leave. There's some weirdness there with her family. We went for ice cream instead."

Calen seemed to miss a beat. "We can have ice cream for dessert," he offered generously after a moment. "What's your favorite flavor?"

Maia stared at him, her mind blank. A few hours ago, she'd been a hairsbreadth from a fate worse than death. And now a ridiculously handsome man was interrogating her about her ice cream preferences.

Be nice and tell him whatever he wants to know.

Feeling slightly surreal and detached, she nodded in agreement with the voice in her head, "Cookies and Cream."

"I like that one, too, although I might like Rocky Road better."

"That's my third favorite," she said, playing with her fork.

"What's the second?" Mike asked.

"Strawberry, but only if it's Häagen-Dazs. If it's Cookies and Cream, it can be anything," she said with a small but genuine smile.

"I think we can do that," Calen said, standing when a timer beeped.

She could hear him moving around the kitchen before calling the concierge downstairs and ordering the ice cream flavors she liked and rocky road for him. He swept back into the dining room a few minutes later with the food. Maia's eyes widened appreciatively when he served her a large pastry-covered slice of beef, which he covered with lots of mushroom gravy.

When the ice cream arrived, Maia declared she couldn't eat another bite, but Calen coaxed her into a small dish. Everything was delicious, and she thanked him profusely.

"Stop thanking me." He laughed.

Maia couldn't remember ever having a nicer meal. And certainly not one in such a lovely place. The dining room, though austere, was beautiful. It belonged in a magazine.

After Mike left, Calen carried her to the living room and started a fire.

"We can get your things tomorrow. I'll take you to your place," he said as he tossed a fuzzy throw over her.

Maia took the blanket gratefully. It wasn't cold, but she still felt chilled from the inside, as if some vital internal organs had been replaced with ice.

"Okay," she said.

She must have looked worried because his face softened.

"I know you're worried about what's going to happen now. I think we should take it one day at time. Tomorrow's Sunday, but come Monday, you probably need to call your school and tell them you're going to be out for a while. Till you're back on your feet again."

Still feeling like she was in some strange dream, she nodded. "If you think that's best."

"What happened?" he asked quietly. "How did they get you?"

Maia lowered her eyes to her lap. Grabbing one of the pillows next to her on the couch, she hugged it close.

"I was out in the woods and I saw those men, the fat one and the huge one with the tattoos. They were burying a body."

He nodded as if her story made sense to him. "What were you doing in the woods?"

"I was collecting specimens for my supervisor's Entomology class. I had just put them in my car and was going to leave when I saw a Long Tailed Skipper. It's not supposed to live so far up north and I wanted to take a picture for the butterfly count."

Calen stiffened and he cocked his head at her. "You were chasing a butterfly?"

"I study them…moths too."

He nodded again, but it looked like he was trying not to laugh and Maia sighed. She had been teased for her looks her whole life. People often compared her to a fairy, and not in a good way. When they found out she studied butterflies on top of that, the teasing could get out of hand. She tensed, waiting for him to say something cutting, but his expression cleared.

"That's perfect," he said softly as if to himself, no trace of a smile in sight.

Calmly he continued to ask her a few questions, details on the men and what their vehicle looked like. She answered his questions but didn't understand why he wanted to know. If he was going to take her to the authorities, he would have done it by now. Instead, she was in his home, having been treated by a private doctor. No policeman would ever know what she had seen.

"You're not asking so you can tell the authorities right?" she asked softly for confirmation.

Calen shook his head with a resigned expression. "I'm afraid not. I know it doesn't seem right or fair, but the best way to keep you safe is to stay quiet. That has to be our priority. I promised the Russians they would never hear from you. The best thing would be to forget you saw anything. That might be hard. Honestly, I don't like it either, but we have to think of your safety."

Maia absorbed that in silence before nodding slowly. She'd been preoccupied with saving her own life, she hadn't even stopped to think about the fact those men were going to get away with murder.

"Will you miss classes if you don't go for a few weeks?" Calen asked when she stayed quiet for too long.

"No, I'm doing research full time. Mostly on the computer right now," she said.

"That's good. You can set up an office here. There's another spare bedroom, but until you can walk around, I can put a desk in your room."

Maia hesitated. "Is that really *my* room?"

Calen stared at her for a moment, an indecipherable expression in his eyes. "For the foreseeable future. And...I think it might be best if people, my family included, think that we're a couple. Maybe even engaged."

Maia panicked. *A couple?* Her with him? Who would believe that?

"Why go so far? Why do we have to pretend?" she asked.

Calen cocked his head to the side. "If the Russians think you're going to be a member of my family, there is less of a chance they'll come after you again."

"Why would they care about that? Is your family important? Are you related to a politician or something?" Maia asked bewildered.

Calen gave her a sharp glance before answering. "My father is Colman McLachlan. That's why I was out there meeting with the Russians. I was doing him a favor."

"I'm sorry," Maia said. "But I don't read the paper. Who is Colman McLachlan?"

CHAPTER 5

as she serious? Did Maia honestly not know about the McLachlans? Calen swallowed his surprise. It had been a long time since anyone had been genuinely ignorant of his background, but Maia was a student. She probably wasn't from around here, and most students were too busy to read the local papers. But his father's exploits weren't always restricted to print.

He laughed. "I guess you don't watch the news, either."

Maia's frown wrinkled her little nose. "Not really."

Calen inhaled deeply, trying to decide what to tell her. In the end, he decided on the truth.

"My father is in organized crime. Like his father before him, and if the stories can be believed, like my great-grandfather before that. Think Don Corleone, but Irish. My family is pretty notorious, and they're completely entrenched in this town. It's a big outfit, but I went another way. I try to play inside the lines. Started my first nightclub at twenty with my best friend Liam. Eventually I bought him out so he could use the profits to open a hotel with his brother Patrick. They're doing pretty well. They own and operate the Caislean chain now. I'm still one of their shareholders."

Maia looked a little green. "*Oh.* I think my supervisor stayed at one of the Caislean hotels during his last conference. He said it was very luxurious. Um, does your father do a lot of business with those people? The Russians?"

"Not as far as I know. They try to stay out of each other's way. They owed him though, big. A distant cousin's kid died. It was their fault, and they offered restitution. It was important, and the relevant parties were busy, so I went to make sure they paid up. I think it's the only thing I've done for the family in like...the last ten years."

"Oh, I thought maybe you were there buying drugs," Maia said with an apologetic wince.

Calen snorted. "I don't do drugs. Well, except alcohol. But hey, I'm Irish."

Maia gave him a tiny shrug, "I thought you might be buying them for your patrons or something."

"No VIP is worth that. I run a clean business. Make a point of it."

"So you're not going to...sell me?"

He laughed aloud. "No."

"Why are you helping me?" Maia's big green-blue eyes were filled with anxiety.

Calen searched for an answer that wouldn't reveal too much. It wasn't like he knew what he was doing. "I saw them bring you in, and I couldn't leave you there."

"Oh. Thank you. It seems so inadequate, but I don't know what else to say except, well, I don't think anyone's going to believe we are a couple," she said hesitantly, plucking at the throw covering her.

"Why not?"

"Have you *seen* you?" she asked in an incredulous tone.

He chuckled. "I've been known to look in a mirror on occasion. What's your point?"

"Have you seen me?"

Since her image was probably still sitting on his desktop, he had to actively stop himself from smiling. Instead, he said, "Yes, I have. No one will question my choice. People generally don't."

"I guess I can believe that..." Maia said, closing her eyes briefly.

She looked tired and completely overwhelmed. Calen questioned her a little more, but his fairy was done for the evening. She fell asleep halfway through a conversation about her research and didn't wake up when he put her to bed.

———

CALEN WAS FLIPPING through one of his prized volumes in the library thinking about the day's events while he waited for the inevitable phone call from his father.

Ice cream, Jesus, he thought, remembering why Maia had disappeared so quickly that day at the club. It was so G-rated it was ridiculous. And it made him feel guilty. He was incredibly attracted to her, but she was such an innocent little thing. He wasn't clean enough to touch Maia. Even if he had been living like a monk lately.

That didn't change the fact that she needed him—despite the strength and fortitude she'd shown today. Most women would have fallen apart. He'd been half expecting her to have some sort of hysterical episode. But even though she was still unsure of him, Maia had gathered herself and carried on with dignity. She had even smiled at him a few times.

It made him feel warm inside, that he'd won a smile from her even after the day she'd had. In fact, the enjoyment she'd gotten out of the meal had been gratifying to see. He hadn't seen anyone eat with such pleasure before.

Almost dying probably does make you appreciate the little things in life.

The phone rang. It was late. His father usually went to bed earlier than this. "What the hell were you thinking boy?" Colman asked, sounding tired.

He rolled his eyes and sighed. "Hello to you too, Da."

"What were you thinking taking one of the Russian's women?"

Calen tensed, the instinct to claim Maia too strong. "She's not theirs. She's just a kid who was in the wrong place at the wrong time."

And she's mine now.

"So Jimmy said. Doesn't matter. You should have let it alone. What happens to her is not your business," Colman said coldly.

"Actually, it is. You see, I know her. She came to the club once," he said, knowing the half-truth would serve him better than an outright lie.

"You went out on a limb for one of your club girls?"

His father sounded disgusted. He had been after Calen to spend more time with someone 'nice' for years, instead of the party girls he was usually seen with. His father, one of the nastiest pieces of work he'd ever known, had no problem with the double standard. He didn't care about getting his or his son's hands dirty, but the women in their lives had to be pristine.

The fact that Darren's wife Mary Margaret had once been a party girl herself had been an issue for the old man. But her willingness to settle down and start squeezing out kids right away had gone far toward earning his goodwill. His father wanted grandkids, a detail Darren was prepared to exploit to curry favor with the old man. Calen had thought it a cold and calculating move at the time, but it was starting to look more and more like a sound strategy.

"Maia isn't a club girl. In fact, she went to Siren once for a birthday party and left early. Not her scene," he said, fingering an image in his book that was close to what he was looking for. "How is Mary Margaret?"

"Okay, for now. They put her on bed rest so she won't go into premature labor. And don't change the subject," Colman said, steel in his voice. "What are you going to do with the girl?"

"I thought that was obvious," Calen said. "I'm going to keep her."

CHAPTER 6

*M*aia woke disoriented and sore. Breathing hurt, and it took her a moment to remember why. Fear coursed through her as she relived the attack in the woods and the ride in the van.

And Calen. She slowed her breathing. She was in Calen's penthouse. He was helping her.

You belong to me now.

Well, maybe he was helping her.

What the hell was he thinking suggesting they pretend to be a couple? Who in the world was going to buy that? Well, if he was the one saying it…

Calen looked like the type of man you didn't question, but she found it hard to believe someone who looked like him would ever be with someone like her. And if she didn't believe it, why would anyone else? Then there was the fact his family was Irish Mob. There was no way *they* would buy it.

She wasn't ugly, but Maia knew she was kind of funny looking. Childhood was excruciating when you looked like an elf. Even now as an adult, she never attracted a lot of male attention. She blended in, and even those rare times when she didn't, she was too shy to do anything about it.

Maia definitely didn't belong on Calen's arm. He was tall, with a swimmer's build and thick dark brown hair with red highlights. In contrast, his eyes were a startling light blue. He was ridiculously attractive. Combined with the fact the he was obviously stinking rich, he surely had women throwing themselves at him all the time.

They would *never* pass for a couple.

Getting out of bed, Maia resolved to deal with that later. For now, it was enough that she was starting to believe he wouldn't hurt her.

CALEN WAITED for Maia to emerge from her room. He'd stayed home the night before to look after her, having his manager at Siren call in with updates. There hadn't been much going on for a Saturday night. The club was settling down into a routine, and he didn't need to be there every night anymore. His other clubs ran just fine without him, although he checked in regularly.

Perhaps Maia would like to visit one or two when she was better. The one in Miami or the one in L.A—both of those were pretty special.

When Maia didn't come out of her room, he decided to bring her breakfast in bed. Getting around was probably still difficult for her. He whipped up some scrambled eggs and toasted an English muffin and put them on a tray with some orange juice. Balancing the tray on one hand, he carried it down the hall and knocked on her door.

"Come in," Maia called out.

He entered, tray in hand. Maia was leaving the bathroom awkwardly on her crutches, and he hurriedly put the tray down.

"Here let me help you," he said, sweeping her up, pretending not to hear her when she objected. He placed her gently on the bed and then brought her the tray. "I'm going to adjust these for you," he said, fiddling with the crutches. "I think they're set for a taller person."

"Thanks," Maia said, her cheeks growing pink as she started on the food.

"You're welcome," he replied, placing the adjusted crutches in her reach near the bed. He liked her easy capacity to blush. "We should go get your things. Do you think you'll be ready to go in an hour?"

"Yes, I can," she said eagerly from around a muffin, making him smile.

"Good. I'll leave you to finish and be back for the tray in a bit," he said as he stood.

Maia was wearing his robe again. It dragged on the ground, which was bad if she was on crutches. He better buy her one in her size immediately. Should he offer to help her change? He was going to have to make sure his housekeeper gave her a hand when she was around, but the woman wasn't working today.

"Um, do you need a hand getting dressed?" he asked, hesitating awkwardly halfway to the door to look back at her.

"No. I'm fine," she said, her blush deepening as she averted her gaze.

"All right," he said.

Then he left to let her eat and get ready in private.

CALEN WAS NOT IMPRESSED when Jay drove them to a shabby looking neighborhood in Allston. It seemed okay…but not great. Mostly families, but appearances were often deceptive in this kind of neighborhood.

As they entered Maia's building, his opinion grew steadily worse. The building's iron door was sound, but its hinges weren't. A crowbar would be enough to get past it. And the front door to her apartment was a joke. One good kick would bust it wide open.

Calen carried Maia inside, again despite her objections. Her face was red when he set her down on an old corduroy couch.

"It's cold in here. Does the heat work?" he asked.

"Yes, but not well. Sometimes it goes out," Maia said apologetically.

"This window doesn't close all the way," Jay said from the windowsill.

Maia's mouth twisted a little. "I know, the wood is a little warped."

"So is the floor," Calen said, looking around the room. "What do you do in winter?" he asked, stepping to the window to examine the gap between the window and the sash.

"I have two electric blankets, one for the couch and one for my bed."

Calen looked away before frowning at his driver. Jay didn't look too happy, either. His little fairy was poor. All of her things were old or used. The coffee table was scarred and worn, probably something she'd salvaged somewhere. The laptop on it was old and beat up. Only the books looked expensive—although most of them had a big yellow USED sticker on the spine.

"Why don't we take the most important things now, like your clothes and books? And these pictures," he said, picking up a framed photo of her and an older woman with the same hair as her. Her features were different, more conventional, but it was clearly her mother. "Do you look like your dad?" he asked curiously.

"I'm not sure. He took off when I was little. Mom didn't keep any pictures of him," Maia said, trying to gather her belongings while balancing on the crutches.

"I'm sorry," he said.

He wanted to help her, but she seemed determined to do it on her own. At least this place was too small for her to be out of reach if she fell.

"It's okay," she murmured as she pulled a few books off a shelf. "I don't think he was around long enough for her to have many pictures."

He didn't know what to say to that. Should he tell her not to feel bad? It wasn't always a blessing to have your father around.

Probably not a good idea.

"What about her? Did she have any family?" he asked, gesturing with the photo.

"No, she was an only child, like me," Maia said softly.

Calen nodded and decided it was time to change the subject. Maia was wilting. "Do you have a suitcase?"

"In the closet."

Since Maia could reach most of her dresser from the bed in the cramped corner, he let her pack her own clothes. Letting her direct him, he took out the ones she wanted from her closet, including the only other coat she had. It was thin and slightly threadbare. The one she had been wearing was newer and thicker, but not by much. And it had been stained and torn in the attack.

He was going to have to buy her a whole new wardrobe. Maybe he should buy her something fur-lined. And some teal-colored dresses.

Something in silk, he thought, warming to the idea of doing some shopping now.

They packed quickly. His fairy didn't have much, a thought that made him uncomfortable. On a hunch, he peeked into her fridge and became unreasonably angry when he saw how empty it was. Putting a lid on his temper, he checked the shelves. The cupboards were a little more full. Non-perishable food, including a few cans of clam chowder. Pleased he'd guessed right about her preferences the day before, he hurried the packing along.

Jay carried Maia's things downstairs in two trips, while Calen carried Maia to the car a little after. After Jay opened the door, he carefully placed her in the backseat before doubling back to give the super on the first floor Maia's notice.

At first, the little prick threatened to withhold her deposit. Once he gave the man his name, he became more cooperative. Sometimes it helped being a McLachlan—saved time at least. After finding out who he was, the super even offered to return the previous month's rent. But Maia wouldn't need it anymore, not while she had him, so Calen told the super to use the rent to get the window and heat fixed for the next poor student. He would send more men to pack up everything else later.

"And make sure the heat and window are fixed before my men come for the rest of Maia's belongings," he ordered coldly as he was leaving. "If you don't, I'll have to come back here. Do yourself a favor and make sure that isn't necessary."

CHAPTER 7

*A*s soon as they returned to the penthouse, he and Jay carried all of Maia's belongings to her room. A new desk had already been delivered for her, but since walking was still difficult, she asked Calen to put the laptop and books on the bed, which was piled high with pillows so she could prop herself up. Then they left her alone to unpack and rest.

When Calen had checked on her that afternoon, he'd found her asleep, surrounded by her books.

A few of them had shifted too close to her. He moved the volumes to the bedside table so they wouldn't dig into her little body while she slept, then went back to his office to look over his latest accounting figures. Things were going pretty well at the clubs, but it was the situation at home that occupied his mind.

Maia was a distraction, but one he didn't mind. He refocused on his work, surprised to find himself whistling a little later.

That night, he and Maia were alone for the first time.

"Do you cook the food?" she asked when he carried her to the dining room again.

She was blushing and avoiding eye contact as he set her down.

With a little time and effort, she could have made it on her crutches, he acknowledged. But he liked holding her too much.

"Only breakfast. My housekeeper slash cook comes in every few days and leaves meals for me to heat up for dinner, and I usually have lunch meetings. I can cook, I'm just usually too busy."

"The eggs were good," she said generously.

"Thanks," he said. "Dinner tonight is lasagna. Do you like Italian?"

"Doesn't everyone?" she said, before shifting in her seat. "Um, has my car been delivered?"

"Yes," he said. "I'm sorry, but one of your windows was broken," he added with a scowl.

"Oh, no. The passenger side window was already broken. I had to park it far from my place because of street sweeping and someone smashed it," she said. "They didn't take anything. There was nothing valuable inside. It's kind of a piece of junk, so it was probably only for the thrill," she added.

Calen smiled in acknowledgement, but it was a little grim as he served the lasagna. Her car *was* a piece of junk. It was currently sitting in one of his car elevators downstairs, a bald contrast to the choice luxury vehicles he had stored there.

"I need to figure out how to get the specimens I collected yesterday to my boss tomorrow," Maia said, toying with her fork.

"I'll take care of it," Calen assured her.

Jay had found several specimen jars and plastic boxes in the backseat of her car. Maia had put leaves and insect food inside them, so the critters were still alive. His driver was keeping them downstairs in the building's security office. One of the security men had already asked if he could keep one of the walking sticks.

He should probably buy her another car, but he didn't like the idea of her driving herself anymore. He should get a driver for her instead. They could use one of his spare cars. He'd already spoken to Maia's new bodyguards, the guys Mike recommended. One of the ex-marines would get here tomorrow before his first meeting. The other man would start by checking out the security situation at Maia's workplace and making changes if needed.

Calen decided to take advantage of the opportunity to get to know his fairy a bit better.

"How old are you?" he asked her between bites.

"Almost twenty-three," she said, sipping a grape juice since she was still on painkillers and couldn't have wine.

He tried not to visibly wince at her answer. Maia was a whole ten years younger than him.

"And where did you grow up?" he asked.

"Outside of Portland. I grew up there, but I haven't been back since my mom died," she said. "There's not much out there for me now and it's expensive to fly," she added in a lower voice.

He nodded understandingly. "Where did the interest in butterflies come from?" he asked as she took another bite of her dish with obvious enjoyment.

Calen suppressed a frown as he watched her. Maia's enthusiasm for the food was still pleasing, but he was starting to wonder. There hadn't been much to eat at her place. The idea that she might have had to prioritize books over food made him edgy, but he kept his face impassive as he waited for her answer.

"Also from my mother," she said eventually. "We hiked a lot in the woods. A class in college solidified my interest, but I actually focus on moths right now."

How adorable. "Sounds interesting," he said.

"Not really," she said with a little shrug. "Not like owning and running a string of nightclubs. That sounds very exotic, going out every night as part of earning your living."

Relaxing in his chair, he shrugged. "That part gets old. I'd much rather stay in these days."

He pushed seconds of lasagna on her and was a little surprised when she thanked him and accepted. Other women never ate around him, preferring to maintain the facade that they didn't eat, fart, or go the bathroom.

More gentle interrogation revealed that Maia was a little bit of a prodigy. She had finished high school early and had attended a small college in Oregon. Her Ph.D. project at Harvard involved studying the diseases that affected moths and butterflies.

"What about your personal life?" he asked, trying not to look too interested.

Maia's brow furrowed. "I don't have much of one right now," she said with a shrug. "I have a few friends, also students. Other than that, I read a lot. And I listen to podcasts when I can't."

"Me, too. I find it easier to keep up with different subjects that way since I don't get much time to read anymore. I subscribe mostly to history and technology podcasts," he replied.

She brightened. "I do, too. And news and humor ones. I listen to way too many. I'm always getting behind."

"That's too easy to do, but I limit mine to a few regularly," he said.

"I should do that too," she said before hesitating. "You mentioned your dad already. What does your mother do?"

"She died when I was little."

Maia turned red. "Oh, I'm sorry."

"It's okay. I don't really remember her. You mentioned yours passed too. How long ago?"

"A few years ago, from cancer. Just before I started school here, actually."

Eager to learn everything he could about her, he asked a few more questions. Her mother had been a clerk in a bank. When she had fallen ill with cancer, the medical bills had eaten all of her savings and then some. Maia was still paying some of the bills off, which explained the state of her apartment and car.

Despite the sometimes sobering details she related, Maia had a way of speaking that intrigued him. She was an engaging conversationalist. A few of the woman he'd dated in the past had been intelligent enough, but they had mainly talked about clothes and television. Maia's interests were a lot more varied, and when she continued to describe her work and life, she made him laugh a few times. It was nice. He hadn't laughed at all in a good long while. Liam had started calling him a dour bastard months ago, but he didn't feel his usual sense of dissatisfaction right now.

Shit. How was he going to explain Maia to Liam? Calen had sworn to his best friend that he would never have anything to do with the McLachlan family business when they were both still in grade school. After a few family-related incidents in high school, Liam had started warning him that it was a slippery slope to go down, and he had never stopped.

And it was true. If his father saw a way into his life, he would exploit it.

Colman had never truly accepted that Calen didn't want to follow in his footsteps, but Calen had drawn a line in the sand. They had argued about it for years, but when he had struck out on his own and built a successful business, Colman hadn't interfered. Not right away anyway. And then Calen had discovered a few of his employees were plants, placed in his clubs by his father. He fired them all immediately. He was never sure what they had been up to, but when he'd threatened to cut off all communication, his father had backed down to avoid losing him altogether.

But if he showed any weakness now, Colman wouldn't hesitate to take advantage. One favor would lead to another and then another if Calen let himself be manipulated. And his father was a master manipulator.

Liam didn't even like the fact that Calen still saw Colman for family gatherings. But taking the meeting had saved Maia, so he couldn't bring himself to regret it.

After ice cream, Maia was nodding off at the table, so he carried her back to bed. This time she was too tired to complain that he shouldn't. She was asleep almost as soon as her head hit the pillow.

Calen spent a long time watching her lying in bed, sleeping the way only the innocent could.

He hoped he could secure her safety, but if he was completely honest with himself, he was selfishly glad that he had a reason to keep her.

On Monday, Maia woke to breakfast in bed again. This time Calen had made her an omelet and toast, along with juice and tea. She'd mentioned liking Ceylon in the mornings yesterday, and now it was on her tray.

"I have a meeting at noon with some investors," Calen said. "I've hired a few of Mike's former special forces buddies who do security work to keep an eye on you while I'm gone. I don't want you to leave the penthouse today, but from now on when you do leave, you don't go anywhere alone. You should get to know Stephens and Davis before you get mobile again. Davis will be here soon," he added, adjusting his tie.

He was dressed for his meeting, intimidatingly handsome in a dark blue suit.

"Okay," Maia whispered, but she looked away as she said it.

"What's wrong?" Calen asked with a frown, sitting on the bed next to her.

She looked at him nervously, her face tight with anxiety. "It's expensive. Bodyguards. The doctor and god knows what else. I don't think I'll ever be able to pay you back, at least not for years," she confessed.

"I don't want you to pay me back. I like having you here," Calen told her, taking her uninjured hand in his.

Maia's eyebrows rose in disbelief.

"*I do,*" he said. "You're good company. Besides, I happen to like having my own personal butterfly biologist." He rose and stood over her. "I don't want you to worry about anything except getting better. "

He dropped a careless kiss on her forehead as his phone buzzed. "Davis is here," he said, "I'll come get you once you're done so you can meet him."

Hmm. There it was again, Maia mused. The suggestion that she belonged to him.

She was pretty sure Calen wasn't going to hurt her. He hadn't done anything to suggest he was anything but what he seemed—a good man. But he was a formidable and forceful one. And he did genuinely seem to enjoy her company, weird as that seemed.

She could still feel his lips on her skin. If she wasn't careful, she was going to start having feelings for her savior.

Maybe she was a sort of novelty for him. A man like him, with the lifestyle she imagined he had, might have gotten jaded. He owned and operated a bunch of nightclubs, and his dad ran an organized crime syndicate. Something told her there weren't a lot of clueless students in his world. Which might be why he was treating her like a shiny new toy.

The question was, what would happen to her once the novelty wore off?

CHAPTER 8

*D*avis was another huge specimen of a man. If Calen hadn't grilled him about his past military history in front of her before he left, Maia would have been afraid of him. But Davis was a complete professional, and before he was done detailing his past work history she was confident in his ability to watch over her. He was as large as the big Russian had been, and probably just as deadly. Maybe more so. And he seemed sympathetic when Calen told him what had happened to her.

Calen had decided to be honest with her guards so they would know exactly what they were up against. Like Mike, Davis didn't like the idea of any man beating on a woman. He frowned ferociously when he saw her bruises and assortment of wrapped appendages. But instead of being frightening, his frown made her feel better about being around him.

After Calen left, she called her supervisor to let him know she was going to be out for a while. He'd been concerned when she'd told him about her 'car accident' but Maia assured him that she was all right.

"Do you need anything?" her boss, Martin Schroeder, asked. "You have all those stairs at your place. Do you need someone to bring you groceries? I'm sure Chang would be happy to drop by."

Chang was her closest friend in the lab.

"No, I don't need anything. I'm staying...with my boyfriend."

Maia felt slightly faint saying the words aloud.

Calen had been clear about everyone in her life thinking they were a couple. He had told her to tell everyone she knew that they were an item. But actually lying to her boss was unnerving. Maia couldn't remember the last time she'd lied to anyone.

"Oh, it must be a new relationship," Dr. Schroeder said, surprised.

"It is. But don't worry. He's taking good care of me," Maia assured him, giving Davis a sidelong glance. "In the meantime, I have everything to work from home for a while. I can crunch the numbers from the last dataset on my laptop, and with access to the digital library, I can catch up on the relevant reading."

"Okay, but let me know if there's anything we can do for you. I know you don't have any family around, so consider us your extended family," he said warmly.

"Thanks, boss," she said gratefully.

Not all supervisors were as nice as hers. After she hung up, she tried to call her friend, Tahlia, but she wasn't able to reach her. After texting a message checking in, she spent the rest of the day organizing her research. Once she plugged in her laptop, she decided to run an internet search on Calen. What she found was more upsetting than she had ever imagined.

Women. Lots and lots of beautiful women. There were brunettes and redheads. A legion of blondes. All of them were voluptuous and most were scantily clad in these online photos. In certain circles, Calen was a celebrity bachelor. His successful string of nightclubs, combined with his family's reputation, gave him the ultimate bad boy cachet.

There were entire websites devoted to Calen's love life. He and his friend Liam and another man that looked like Liam were photographed in numerous hotspots, always with a gorgeous woman on their arm. Sometimes *two*. There were more pictures of Calen on French or German websites with another man called Sergei whom she thought he'd mentioned at dinner last night.

What he should have mentioned were the women. Though it didn't look like Calen had been linked to any of them for long, those images of so many barely-dressed women were now burned into her brain. No one was ever going to believe that Calen had given up all of that for someone like her.

Feeling slightly sick to her stomach, Maia proceeded to bury herself in work. She tried to distract herself with statistics, but couldn't shake the feeling of impending doom that was starting to become familiar.

CALEN WAS eager to come home to Maia. Getting home to an empty apartment had become distinctly unsatisfying since Alex's wedding, but now he knew someone was waiting for him, and it felt good. It felt even better knowing the person waiting for him was his fairy.

He had expected to like Maia based on her appearance, but her natural sweetness and modest demeanor were even more endearing than her looks. Eager to spend another evening getting to know her, he set down his packages on the couch. He'd bought a few things for her, including a new laptop and cashmere coat, and he couldn't wait to watch her open her gifts.

Calen already had two different personal shoppers picking out a new wardrobe for Maia. And in addition to today's gifts, he also had all of the personal belongings left in her car. There hadn't been much aside from her empty specimen jars, which he had stored downstairs. As for the car itself, it was being hauled away for scrap tomorrow. Maia could take his town car from now on if she needed to go out. He would drive his Tesla for a while until his New York town car arrived for his personal use.

Calen waited for Davis' report before he dismissed the man to go to Maia's room to say hello. She looked pale and her smile was a little weak.

"Are you okay, doll? Are you feeling worse? Should I call the doctor?"

"Oh, no. I'm fine. A little tired," she said, a touch wanly.

Scowling slightly, he examined her cheek and the traces of her black eye. "The swelling has gone down," he said, running a fingertip gently down her cheek. "Maybe you should take a nap before dinner. Did you call your supervisor?"

"Yeah, I told him I was staying with my new boyfriend like you said. He was a little surprised, but okay. He's a nice boss," she said, opening her hands and resting them in her lap.

Calen leaned back and cocked his head at her, "Did you tell him my name?"

"No."

"He probably won't be as okay with it when he finds out who I am," he said derisively. "I don't suppose he avoids the newspapers like you do?"

Maia took exception to that. "I don't *avoid* them. I just don't think to read them unless something big is going on."

"How big is big?" he asked.

"Hurricane or terrorist attack big," she said a little sheepishly.

He grinned, and she sighed and looked down with another of her cute blushes. "What about your coworkers and boss? Do you think they know who I am?" he asked.

She shrugged. "Someone will recognize your name, I'm sure," she said in an oddly fatalistic tone.

"Well, don't let them get you on the defensive," he said quietly. "They're going to try and talk you out of seeing me."

"I don't know if that's true, but if they say something, I'll think of something to put them off. I know what's at stake. And thank you again for doing this for me. I know you're really putting yourself out," she said, her incredible eyes filled with anxiety.

"I'm not being put out," he said, bending down to give her a quick kiss on the forehead. "Dinner is lobster potpie. Does that sound good?"

"Sure," she said, growing pinker.

He shouldn't enjoy making her blush quite so much.

"I'll come get you when it's ready," he said, leaving before she could reply.

"THIS IS the first time I've had lobster. I like it," Maia said, finishing her potpie with gusto.

Calen was watching her with an amused expression. "I'm glad you like it. I get a kick out of watching you eat. You enjoy your food more than anyone I've ever known. It's fun to watch."

Maia made a face. "When you live off of PB&J sandwiches, most anything is an improvement," she joked weakly, turning to look at the room again.

It was beautiful. *He must have had a decorator design it.* When she looked back at Calen, his smile had dropped off his face, giving it a stern forbidding look.

Intimidated, her chest tight, she asked, "What's wrong?"

Calen's head lowered slightly, and all expression wiped off his face. But his voice was clipped when he finally said, "I just don't like hearing about all the things you did without. In addition to a warm winter coat, I can add a smartphone, a reliable car, and now apparently decent meals to the list. I saw how little food you kept at your place, but I was hoping that simply meant you ate out a lot. But you didn't, did you?"

Surprised and startled, Maia was quiet. Calen sounded genuinely angry. She stared at him apprehensively. As though noting her disquiet, he made a visible effort to soften his features.

"Sorry. I'm not angry at you. Just your situation," he said eventually.

Maia pursed her lips. "I don't *have* a situation. I didn't always have time to cook. And I was on a budget, so I didn't get a lot of fancy stuff. But it's not like I was starving," she added a little defensively, holding the fork tightly in her hand.

"And was this budget necessary because of all the medical bills your mother left? Don't you still owe almost another twenty grand in addition to your college loans because of her medical expenses?"

Maia's stomach tightened. How did he know the exact amount? "Did you run a credit check on me or something?"

Calen looked like he was starting to regret starting this conversation. "I paid off those bills today. You don't have to worry about them anymore. I also opened you new savings and checking accounts at my bank. There's plenty of money in them to get whatever you might need. I told them to rush your new credit cards. They should arrive by the end of the week."

Maia's mouth dropped open. "Why did you do that? I'll never be able to pay you back!"

Calen scowled. "You don't have to pay me back. Maia, you're living with me now. Under my roof and my protection. I pay your bills from now on. I also buy your clothes, and the food you eat. I even buy the toiletries you use. I get to decide what you smell like because I choose your soap and shampoo. But you're right. This isn't free for you. In fact, I'm going to be asking for a lot from you."

Oh god, here it comes. "What do you want from me?"

The words came out a little garbled, she sounded like she was choking. Calen shifted in his seat uncomfortably. He put his hands together and templed them under his chin. Eventually he leaned back.

"I want you to consider making our fake relationship a real one. I think we should get married."

CHAPTER 9

"*What?*" Maia stared at him dumbfounded.

"I said I think we should get married. And have a real marriage. Sharing the same bed and the same life. Have kids. The whole nine yards."

"What?" she repeated, eyes flaring wide.

The slight tinge of panic in her voice was not flattering for Calen. He tensed in his seat. "It would be a good life," he reassured her. "You would want for nothing. It's the best way to keep you safe, and I would get a wife whose company I enjoy."

He masked his disappointment with her reaction with his habitual stern facade.

"Why would you do that?" she breathed, still in shock.

"Because I want to," he said, frowning at her.

She shook her bright head in disbelief. "You can't possibly make that kind of sacrifice and not come to regret it!"

Calen cocked his head at her. What did she mean by that?

"It's not a sacrifice for me…"

"Of course it is! I've googled you. None of the women you have ever been photographed with look like me. Not even in the same ball-park. They were all gorgeous, and they all had these huge—" she cut herself off and gestured wildly with her hands in front of her small pert breasts.

Relieved, Calen's tension fell away, and he laughed aloud. When Maia frowned at him, he passed a hand over his mouth until he stopped.

"Is that your only reservation?"

"*No!*" she said, leaning in with an incredulous expression.

"But it's your biggest one?" he asked.

"There are a million reasons why it won't work. Your family for one."

His temperature dropped by several degrees. "What about my family?"

"They won't ever believe you willingly chose me."

Some of the warmth trickled back. "They will once I get you pregnant."

Maia went a little pale.

Uh oh, Calen thought. "Do you not like kids?"

If she didn't, his plans would become complicated.

Maia opened and closed her mouth a few times. *Probably shouldn't have sprung it on her like that.* Pouring himself more wine, he waited for her to calm down enough to respond. He was half way done with his glass before she finally spoke.

"I do...I love babies, but I didn't think I'd ever be having any. At least not so soon. Do you want kids? *Soon?*"

The last was a breathy little whisper.

Calen wanted to hug her, but he didn't think that was going to help calm her down. Instead, he settled for patting her hand. He didn't want to scare her any more than he already had, but he had to be honest with her.

"Sooner rather than later would be best, I think. The Russians and my family would know better than to mess with you then...but I do understand that it would be better for our marriage if we waited a bit."

"Our marriage," Maia repeated, wide-eyed. She still looked panicked. "What about sex?" she asked, her voice high.

Calen held back a laugh. That wouldn't help his cause. "Last time I checked, it was a pre-requisite for having children," he said evenly.

Maia frowned, and her shell-shocked expression morphed into an annoyed one. It was adorable. "I mean, do you think you would be happy...doing that with me?"

Calen leaned forward, startling Maia and making her edge back in her seat. He reached out to her to touch her unbruised cheek.

"I'm going to be *very* happy doing that with you," he confessed, his breath fanning her cheek. Maia's breath stuttered a little and she turned a rosy red. It was charming. "I find you incredibly attractive," he added.

She stared at him like he was a crazy person. "What happens when you get bored?" she whispered.

"What makes you think I'm going to get bored?" he asked, drawing her chair closer to him.

"*Because.* I don't have—" she gestured to her chest again, and he did laugh this time, right before he kissed her.

MAIA'S first kiss was startling. Calen was physically closer to her than any man had ever been—or even any boy. Heart hammering, she felt enveloped in his body heat. Her skin was tingling in response. She almost jumped out of her skin when the tip of his tongue began to trace her lower lip. Until he bit it—not hard, but it surprised her. She yelped before she could stop herself, and that teasing tongue slid inside her mouth.

Heat coursed through her body and pooled in the places she usually ignored. Her head was spinning. She felt faint, yet hyperaware of each sensation at the same time. Calen pulled her in close, his hands resting on her hips. The heat and pressure of them seemed strange and alien on her body, until he moved one of them to caress and cup her left breast. Startled, she broke the kiss to look down at his hand. But he didn't stop stroking her.

"These," he whispered, "these are absolutely perfect."

He pinched her nipple between his thumb and forefinger through her shirt, and smiled when she sucked in her breath. Her blush felt impossibly hot, and her lips burned.

"Are you done eating? Want dessert?" he asked, tweaking her nipple a last time before finally removing his hand.

She gave a little gasp, and his grin turned predatory.

"Not hungry," she said when he looked at her expectantly.

"Okay then," he said, swooping down to carry her to her room.

He put her down on the bed and sat next to her. He fingered a lock of her hair absently as she held her breath.

"I know you're feeling overwhelmed right now. You probably think you don't have a choice. And I'm not going to lie to you...things would be much easier if you agreed to go along with my plans. But I don't think you would regret it if you did. We can make this work. However, if you feel strongly that this isn't right for you, we can figure something else out. Think it over."

With that suggestion, he rose from the bed and left her alone with her racing thoughts.

CHAPTER 10

$\mathcal{M}$aia woke up to a cheerful, middle-aged Hispanic woman cleaning out her closet. Mrs. Portillo, Calen's cook and housekeeper, introduced herself and told her what a pleasure it was to meet the future Mrs. McLachlan. Flushing with embarrassment, Maia thanked her.

She hadn't spent much time thinking about Calen's request. It was like her mind refused to process it. But even if she decided not to go through with it, Calen wanted everyone to believe they were engaged. At least for now.

She was confused when Mrs. Portillo started making a pile of her belongings next to the closet. "What are you doing with my clothes?" she asked.

"I'm making room at the Master's request. Your new clothes are here," Mrs. Portillo said with a satisfied look at the pile.

"What new clothes?" Maia asked blankly.

"Some lovely new dresses. And some nice winter clothes, too," the woman said, fingering Maia's thin jacket with a frown.

Her other warmer coat had been torn during the attack in the woods. Calen had thrown it out, despite her protest that she could have it mended.

"Oh."

Maia processed that quietly. Calen's words about her clothes and toiletries came back to her. He wanted to be the one to decide how she dressed, even how she smelled.

On impulse she asked, "Did he ask you to call him Master?"

"No, but it is proper, and he likes it. He likes things just so," the beaming housekeeper replied.

Well, that's telling, Maia thought.

Calen clearly liked control. He was a textbook example of a dominant alpha male, the kind that would actually help a damsel in distress. But there was more to it than that. Having someone to control, someone dependent on him, was probably a very appealing thing to a man like him. Her presence in his household was starting to make a lot of sense.

MAIA SAT on the large leather couch in the living room, surrounded by new clothes. Dazed, she fingered the fine silk of a turquoise dress close to the color of her eyes. There were probably tens of thousands of dollars worth of haute couture here. The camel-colored cashmere coat alone had to be worth a thousand at least. Probably more. And all of it was in her size.

Mrs. Portillo handed her a few more boxes with an exclusive label. When she opened them, she blushed hotly. It was lingerie—a lot of it. Silk and lace. Even some satin. All lovely. Nothing terribly risqué, but certainly more daring than anything she owned. In fact, she didn't own anything that looked remotely like any of these things.

Her underwear was like her clothes. Plain and serviceable. Some of it was noticeably worn. But these clothes were so beautiful, all with a modern romantic look; the kind of things fashion magazines would dress models they photographed in woods—dream gowns and lingerie for faux wood nymphs. She was starting to get the idea Calen wanted to wrap her in luxury while indulging certain fantasies. It made her feel special and anxious at the same time.

After Maia looked over the clothes, Mrs. Portillo suggested she change into one of the filmy silk dresses as a special surprise for Calen. She let the woman help her bathe. Her fingers felt better, but her ankle was still painful. Mrs. Portillo helped her rewrap it as well as her ribs. The housekeeper had been told the car accident version of events, and she was so sympathetic that Maia started to feel guilty for lying to her.

After she changed and Mrs. Portillo fussed over her hair, the kind woman made her a sandwich. Maia ate with heavy eyes and then moved over to the couch in the living room to rest. She was tempted to ask the housekeeper for a fire, but was too tired. Instead, she picked up the fuzzy throw Calen kept out on the couch and curled underneath it for a nap.

Multiple male voices and laughter scared Maia awake. Disoriented, she hugged the fuzzy blanket closer to her chest, her wide eyes meeting the equally startled expressions of the two tall and imposing men who'd just entered the living room.

They were both broad and muscular, and dressed incredibly well in suits that had to be custom made to fit their frames so perfectly. One was holding a bottle of liquor. They looked like a windblown advertisement for an exclusive brand of whiskey.

"Well, what have we here?" the younger of the two men said.

He had light brown hair and brown eyes that crinkled at the corner, like he laughed a lot. The other one was a few years older, with darker hair and eyes, but he had similar features to the other visitor. Except he didn't look like he *ever* laughed.

"Hello," Maia croaked, her voice still sleepy.

The younger one smiled at her and stepped closer. Maia instinctively shrank back, her heart pounding. They both noticed and frowned. The older one frowned more deeply when he zeroed in on the bruises that marred her face and the crutches lying at her side.

"Who are you and what happened to you?" he asked Maia in a no-nonsense gravelly voice.

"I'm Maia Dahl. I'm Calen's fiancée. I—I was in a car accident."

Both men gave each other startled looks, and the younger one laughed. "Calen wouldn't get engaged without telling us. Who are you really?"

Realization struck, and Maia felt the blood draining from her face, "Oh, you're Liam and Patrick," she said weakly.

She should have recognized them from their pictures on all those web sites. As though puzzled by her reaction, the men gave each other another pointed look while Maia tried to rack her brain to remember what Calen was going to tell his best friends about her.

She couldn't remember if he'd said he was going to tell them the truth or their cover story...which if everything went as he planned, wouldn't be a story at all. Watching the men anxiously, she wished Calen would get home.

"So you're engaged to Calen," Liam said in a tone that clearly indicated he didn't believe her. "How did you two meet?"

The way he said *engaged* practically put air quotes around it.

"I, uh...at his club. I was there with some girlfriends."

"A girls night, huh? And call me Trick. Everyone does," Patrick said, still smiling as he pulled up a chair to sit across from her.

Liam didn't smile though, which made her nervous.

"Oh, don't worry about him," Patrick said, catching her wary glance. "He's a naturally suspicious bastard. Calen told us he had news, we just weren't expecting...this. Can't blame us for being a little surprised. You don't seem like Calen's type. Not that he has a type. Not really."

Maia's dismay must have showed on her face because Liam shifted and gave her a penetrating look.

"Actually, if you go by what's in his library, she's exactly his type," he murmured.

Patrick looked confused and then beamed like he had suddenly remembered it was Christmas. "His collection. Oh, my god yes!" he shouted excitedly, so loud Maia jumped.

"What collection?" she asked.

She must have been very pale now, picturing a pile of DVD's of teen and barely-legal porn. Her question went unanswered. The three of them simply sat there and stared at each other until the elevator dinged behind them.

Calen, face creased with worry, rushed into the room. "What is going on here?"

CHAPTER 11

*C*alen practically ran upstairs when Davis reported that Liam and Patrick had dropped by. They were on his approved list, and their prints were on the finger print lock, but he hadn't had a chance to tell them about Maia yet. He'd been procrastinating, knowing he would have to tell Liam the truth about how he actually met her.

He'd planned on introducing Maia to his friends over drinks, keeping it casual and lighthearted until he had a chance to take the guys aside and explain. But now he couldn't do casual. Maia looked scared. Her face was white...but that didn't stop Trick from looking at her a touch too warmly for his taste.

He wasn't sure how long they'd been interrogating his fairy, but he was putting a stop to it right now. Maia was still recovering, and these two overbearing asses were a lot to take even on a good day. And yes, those overbearing asses were his best friends. Usually he was twice as bad, but he tried to rein himself in around Maia.

Calen ignored the two men while he checked her temperature with his palm. "You look pale, nymph. Are you feeling okay? Should I call the doctor?"

"I'm fine," she said weakly, shifting the blanket down to her waist.

His eyes warmed appreciatively when he saw what she was wearing, but he tamped down his sudden arousal. They had company.

"Why don't you rest in your room until dinner is ready while I talk to Liam and Trick," he said, picking her up. As he swept Maia out of sight, he called over his shoulder to his friends. "I'll be right back."

She looked so beautiful in her new dress, despite the faint bruises on her cheek. It made him want to linger, but the guys were waiting, so he gave Maia a quick kiss and deposited her gently on the bed.

"I don't think they believed me when I said I was your fiancée," she whispered with a little grimace. "I wasn't sure if you had told them the truth or not."

He sighed. "I'm going to tell them now. Don't worry about it. Just rest. You look beautiful, by the way," he said giving her another quick kiss before leaving the room.

Liam was waiting in the hallway, Maia's crutches in hand. "What the hell is going on?" he asked with his customary bluntness.

Calen rolled his eyes and took the crutches, putting them next to the door before walking back to Trick. Liam followed him out to the living room. He stopped to pour himself a tall glass of whiskey from the bar.

"Why is your 'fiancée' lying about where she met you?" Liam demanded.

He sighed. Liam was good at reading people, and Maia was a terrible liar. Calen loved that about her—except right now.

"Because she *was* lying," he said, passing a tired hand over his face.

He was not looking forward to this.

"Why would she lie?" Trick asked with a frown, his usual devil-may-care attitude sank below his brother's oppressively serious one.

"Come into the office. I don't want Maia to hear us if she gets up," Calen said, leading the way.

The men followed him without a word. Reaching his sanctuary, he dropped into one of the leather armchairs he'd arranged into a conversational nook next to the small fireplace.

His office doubled as a library. It had an impressive assortment of leather bound first editions as well as several weighty financial tomes.

Books on philosophy, the natural sciences, and art lined the walls. It was one of those rare private libraries that was actually used. But his favorite and most personal collection of books was kept in the shelves behind the desk. Someday he would have to show those volumes to Maia.

Liam waited until Trick helped himself from the bar across from the library doors. He sat in the chair nearest the unlit fireplace while his brother took the other.

"Well? Why did she lie?" Liam demanded.

Calen's shoulders tensed as he braced himself. "Because I told her to."

There was a pointed silence. Calen took another fortifying drink. Liam was a stubborn and irritating bastard, but a loyal friend, and he did owe him an explanation.

"I took a meeting for my father. A meeting with a Russian crew, the Komarovs."

The explosion wasn't long in coming. And it wasn't only Liam standing over him and shouting. Trick joined in the fun.

He is starting to resemble his older brother more and more every day.

Calen let them vent for a while and then waved them into silence. "All right, enough!"

Liam shook his head. "What the hell were you thinking?" he asked in disbelief, running his hand through his hair.

"It was a one-time thing, and it's over now."

When Liam tried to interrupt, Calen cut him off. He explained about the reason for the meeting and his father and Darren's inability to make it after the painstaking effort it had taken to set up. Darren's wife, Mary Margaret, had been fine in the end. She was on bed rest for the rest of her pregnancy, but both mother and baby were expected to get through the delivery with no problems.

"You know how I felt about that shit when it all went down," Calen reminded them. "I wanted to stick it to those assholes myself," he added, taking a sip of his drink.

"That's how these things start," Liam berated him. "For Christ's sake, you saw the Godfather," he bit out.

"I saw it, and I still don't regret going. I will never do anything like it again, but I can't regret it because that's how I got Maia."

That shut them up.

"How *did* that happen?" Patrick asked.

Calen told them about Maia chasing a butterfly in the woods. They thought it was amusing until he told them how she stumbled upon the men burying a body. He explained about Timur and Viktor and how they had run her down like some sort of animal.

"They were going to kill her?" Trick asked, looking green.

Trick was the most chivalrous man Calen knew. He was always looking out for the women in their circle. Any suggestion that one was being hassled or abused in any way was enough to get him going. But none of the women they knew had ever been in danger. Not like Maia had been.

"Yeah. They were. But not right away," Calen growled. "Timur is the worst kind of sick shit. I'd heard about him before this. He gets off on...on cutting girls up while he rapes them. When the girls the Russian's run get out of line, they give them to Timur to punish. They let him do what he wants when they want to make an example of someone—but he enjoys it. I don't want to think about what he would have done to Maia if he had been given time."

"Is she okay?" Liam asked gravely.

His attitude changed after hearing the truth about Maia, but Calen had been expecting that. When it came down to it, Liam was also an overprotective pushover when it came to women. Not the ones he was dating of course, but friends and family. It probably came from raising their sister from the time he should have been out at high school parties. Liam and Patrick's parents had passed away in a car accident during their junior year. Liam was the oldest, almost two years older than Trick and nine years older than their sister Maggie.

Their deaths had been hardest on Liam. He was the man of the family, and as a result, he'd been acting as though he was forty since they graduated high school. His concern for Maia was genuine, though, and Calen was grateful for that overprotective streak in his best friend.

"She is," he said. "I got her out of there in time before they could...you know," he said, waving a little drunkenly, not wanting to say it aloud.

"Well, that's good. So what are you going to do with her now?" Trick asked, taking a big drink.

Calen straightened in his chair. "I've decided to keep her."

"What does that mean?" Trick asked, dribbling whiskey from his mouth in surprise.

"I mean I'm going to marry her," Calen announced. "If she decides to go through with it, that is."

After a pregnant pause, Liam cleared his throat. "This is for real, right? It's not a joke? Or is it something you think you have to do to protect her?"

Calen shook his head. "I want this. More than I ever thought I would."

His friends absorbed that in silence. He and Liam had been friends since he was five. They were each other's first friend. And once they were old enough for the small age difference between the brothers to become insignificant, he and Trick had grown close. The three of them had been through a lot together. Even more than him and Sergei, who felt like his twin sometimes.

"Are you sure? Are you prepared to throw away your whole single life for this girl? One that you don't know at all?" Liam said, his cynicism breaking through.

Calen sat back. "What am I throwing away? I'm tired of being alone. Partying at the clubs is boring as shit these days. That's why I don't want to build a new one at the Caislean. I can't even work up the energy for that, and you know I love that place." He put down his drink and decided to be as honest as could. "I want someone to come home to, someone to care about and vice versa. And Maia is special. I can feel it in my bones. It's true, I think she'll be safer as my wife, but I happen to want a wife. As far as I'm concerned, we have as good a shot as any other couple that met under traditional circumstances."

The brothers exchanged an unreadable glance.

"*Okay*," Trick said. "So what's she like?"

Calen relaxed and told them all about his fairy. Her smile. The quirky little sense of humor that he was only now starting to see. Her brains and that sweet manner she had. And her modesty. Also, the fact she was apparently a terrible liar. Trick and Liam were shaking their heads and laughing at him by the time he was done.

"Shut up, you stupid gits," he growled, slamming back the last of his drink before starting to laugh, too.

"So you genuinely want her," Liam said, leaning forward in his chair.

"I do," Calen said, his laughter subsided. "I can make her happy."

"Of course you can," Trick said lightly.

"No...you don't get it. Maia doesn't get to choose. She's stuck with me. Whether she likes it or not. Whereas I know I want her, I don't know if she wants me. But even if she doesn't, it's not like she can go back to her old life."

Trick stopped laughing.

"I'm sure you're not going to have a problem on that score. When has a woman ever failed to fall all over you?" Liam asked pragmatically.

Calen shrugged. "Maia's not like the women who hang around us. She's completely different. That's the whole fucking point."

Liam waved dismissively. "Then persuade her. I don't think it will be that hard. What is the alternative? I guess you could send her away. Far away," he suggested, but Calen shook his head.

"They would go looking for her once they realized she wasn't with me. The only way to make sure she's safe is to keep her close. Timur is fucking psychotic. The things he does to girls, what I've heard about him, it's all pretty fucked up. Maia won't be safe until it's drummed into his and all those other assholes' heads that she's no threat to them. That she's protected."

"Whatever you need man, we're here to help," Trick said.

"Well, for the moment, you can make my girl feel welcome at dinner," Calen said, getting back up and motioning for them to follow him.

DINNER WAS AN EXPERIENCE FOR MAIA. She'd never spent much time in the company of the opposite sex, and now she was faced with wall-to-wall beefcake. Calen was the most handsome, but Liam and Trick (as Patrick insisted he be called) were intimidatingly good-looking as well.

She knew that most women would give their right arm to be in her shoes that night. Though they were somewhat overwhelming, especially Liam, they were kind.

Once Calen had assured her he'd told them everything, she'd relaxed, allowing the collective charm of the men wash over her. She was uncomfortable lying and knowing she didn't have to anymore calmed her nerves. The wine Calen kept plying her with now that she'd stopped taking painkillers also helped. Eventually, she was laughing at the stories Liam and Trick told her about Calen, despite the fact it hurt her face a little to laugh. But she couldn't help it. Trick was a master storyteller, and his tales of misspent youth and all the trouble they used to get into as boys were hilarious.

She even made them laugh, too, which she found surprising since she was usually so shy in company. They left promising to introduce her to their sister Maggie, making her feel like she was being set up on a play date.

Maia kicked herself for not having the guts to mention Calen's DVD collection while they were still there. Although calling attention to it in front of them might have been worse.

"Don't feel like you have to be friends with Maggie or anything. They're just excited to welcome you into the fold," Calen said, coming back to the table after he walked the men to the elevator.

"I wouldn't mind meeting her. I've been so busy with school, that other than Tahlia, I haven't made friends outside of work people."

"Tahlia?"

"The birthday girl, the reason we went to Siren. I mentioned her before. She's a third-year graduate student in the math department. Although we're not that close," she tacked on honestly.

Calen looked confused. "Why not?"

Maia opened her hands in a questioning gesture. "I'm not sure. She's...a little reserved. I mentioned that there's a bit of weirdness with her family. I think it makes her a little closed off. But she's nice to me and includes me in stuff sometimes. I met her at a graduate mixer, a wine and cheese tasting."

"Have you told her about me yet?"

"I haven't gotten ahold of her. But I texted her and will see her on campus when I go back."

Calen's expression became serious. "Yes, we should talk about how that's going to work. Will you come sit with me in the living room? I can make a fire."

Maia nodded with a faint smile. "Sure. I love your fireplace. Real wood fires smell so good."

Calen gave her one in return. "Yeah, I like them, too."

THEY WERE SITTING by the fire, close but not quite snuggling. Calen could feel the contentment he'd been searching for nearly in his grasp. He wanted to reach out and pull Maia close, but he didn't want to overwhelm her...or hurt her ribs. Instead, he talked to her about his concerns.

"The building you work in will be hard to secure. It has too many entrances. Though there is supposed to be key card access only, there are open hours for undergrads to come in without one. Not to mention the fact that your building connects to the ones on either side of it with some underground tunnels. Davis and Stephens have some concerns about them, but I think the best we can do is tap into the existing security feeds and add a few of our own cameras in the current blind spots. Davis and Stephens will watch the exterior. One of them can monitor the cameras from a nearby van while the other patrols. Another two guys, Marks and Ellis, will trade off with them periodically when the other two need some downtime, but your security will chiefly be handled by Davis and Stephens. They're used to working together."

"You're going to add cameras? Secretly? What if people find them?" Maia asked, her hands twisting in the little blanket thrown over her lap.

"Pretend you know nothing about them. You may have to practice; cause right now your face gives away your every thought," he said with a lift of his brows. "I realize lying isn't something you would normally do, but it's the lesser of evils. Unless of course Davis sits on you all day, waiting in your office for you."

"Oh, no! That would never work," Maia exclaimed. "I share a tiny office with two other graduate students. A massive bodyguard would disrupt work for everyone. It's a small lab."

"That's what I thought you were going to say. Well, on occasion the guards will be there to pick you up. They will only come inside if they think there's a threat or if you asked them too. We'll have to take your supervisor into our confidence when you go back. But don't mention the cameras."

"Okay," she said slowly. "Do you think there is a genuine threat there? Am I putting my coworkers in danger?"

"If all goes as well, the Russians will drop it. But it would be best if they had a reason to," Calen said softly.

"Like getting married to their rival's son?"

He studied Maia in the firelight. Her eyes were huge in her pale, heart-shaped face. He felt bad for pushing her, but the alternative— living platonically with someone so tempting—was unacceptable to him. It would be torture. And he'd crack sooner rather than later. He wouldn't be happy until Maia was in his bed. At least this way she'd have a ring on her finger and his name to protect her.

"My father isn't their rival, exactly. More like a competitor in a superior position. And there is no way they would risk outright war if you joined our family. Marriage is the most expedient way," he said in a low voice.

Maia's head lowered and she blinked several times. Calen felt another flash of guilt before pushing it away. He was doing what was best for her. From her frequent blushes and the way she looked at him, he knew she found him attractive. In time they could build on that. But she did have an alternative and he would be a complete asshole if he didn't let her choose.

"If you can't face marriage to me you can run...change your identity. I will help you. But you'll have to leave everything."

He didn't see another alternative. Not one that would work as well for the two of them as marriage.

For a moment, Maia was quiet. Too long. Threads of disappointment were starting to pool in his gut when she finally shook her head.

"I don't think I could bring myself to do that," she said with a pained look. "I don't have a whole lot in my life except for my studies. I've spent my entire life working to be where I am now. I couldn't just give it up and live with myself," she said with a heavy sigh, collapsing on the couch cushion more deeply. "Of course, if we do things your way, I'm not sure how you would live with *me*. Are you seriously willing to marry me? What if I drive you crazy? What if you meet someone else? Is that why you think kids are a good idea? If we had one and you wanted to end this, would my status as your child's mother be enough to keep me alive?"

Man, she'd given this a lot of thought. "I haven't considered things not working out between us because I think they will," he said softly as he caressed her cheek with his index finger.

It was hard to see her blush in the dim light, but he could feel her skin heat under his touch.

"You can't blame me for planning for the worst case scenario. Don't forget I looked you up online," she said with a wry twist of her lips.

He laughed. "I haven't forgotten. But I'll be honest...I haven't been happy with my life lately. I'm tired of the scene. Of women who wanted to be on my arm or in my bed in order to be seen with me or for money. It gets old. I want something else now."

"And you think *I* can give it to you?" she looked at him in disbelief, eyes huge.

Those eyes of hers were so expressive. He loved their unusual teal color and the way they complemented her orange-gold hair. Calen could practically see the wheels turning in her head, and he wanted to smile at her hesitant naiveté. But that would be unfair of him.

"I do," he said with a straight face. "And I think you should let me prove it."

"How?"

"A trial period. You're getting better. Healing. Once you are...I'm going to want to touch you. So I should. And you should touch *me*."

Maia looked at him, slightly open-mouthed.

"Oh." She ran a hand through her hair before letting it fall on the blanket, where it twisted with its partner. "I guess if you want to try, that might be smart. Then we would know for sure if we're compatible."

The dimness of the light ceased to matter, he could see Maia's blush clearly now.

Satisfaction coursed through him. "I do want to try," he said, reaching out to take her hand. "It's the best way to figure out if my plan would work. If it doesn't, then you can give more thought to leaving town. Maybe witness protection. But that should be your last resort."

He didn't want to scare her by telling her what he knew about Timur. Even in a program like witness protection there were no guarantees she would be safe. But that wasn't going to be an issue. If she said yes to getting physical, he'd make sure she never wanted to leave.

Maia didn't answer right away. After a few more moments of blinking and staring at the fire, she swallowed heavily and nodded.

"Okay. A trial period."

He finally let his satisfaction show. With a slow easy grin, he put his arm around her and drew her closer to his side. He wanted to kiss her again, but Maia was still fragile. Pushing away his arousal, he talked to her instead about her work until she grew tired and went to bed.

Calen stayed awake long after, flipping through the volumes in his collection.

This time he was looking for illustrations that included butterflies.

CHAPTER 12

*T*he next few weeks were like some surreal dream. Maia worked out with a physical therapist that came to the penthouse. They used the penthouse's gym, a state of the art facility that even had its own swim spa—a Jacuzzi tub with a motorized lap pool for one person at the other end.

When she wasn't working on her recovery, she used her laptop to do her research and catch up on her reading.

Calen came and went at irregular hours, taking meetings and checking on his clubs. He made an effort to be home at a regular hour for dinner, a meal they would always share. It felt very domestic. Calen would kiss her often...albeit gently. He wasn't physically demanding, but she could tell that he hadn't been lying when he said he found her attractive.

Maia was completely caught off guard the first time she noticed he was aroused around her. Perhaps she shouldn't have been, given what he was proposing, but she was still surprised.

She'd had a long workout with the physical therapist that afternoon. The therapist suggested Maia make use of the hot tub as part of her recovery. After he left, Maia changed into a bathing suit. She hadn't even owned one before her attack, but a few skimpy bikinis had been included with all the clothes Calen had bought her. Trying to ignore how she looked, Maia changed into the darker of the swimsuits, a green one that covered more of her than the delicate white one also provided.

The controls for the spa weren't difficult to figure out. Maia sank into the hot water with a sigh. She was sitting on one of the shallower seats in the tub; the bubbles barely covering her. Her hair was piled high on her head to avoid getting it wet while she relaxed in the soothing heat. Stretching her sore ankle far above the level of the water, she massaged her leg with both hands until she heard a noise. Letting her leg drop and turning swiftly, she was startled to see Calen watching her from the doorway.

"You're back early tonight," she said shyly. "Mrs. Portillo won't have dinner ready till seven."

When he just nodded, she grew nervous. The quiet stretched so long she wondered if something was wrong.

"Is everything okay?" she asked tentatively.

"Uh, yes. Yes, of course," Calen said after a little cough. "I'm going to take a shower before dinner."

"You still have time. Would you like a soak?" she asked gesturing to the hot tub politely, despite her anxiety about having him join her.

Calen avoided looking directly at her, but he shifted uncomfortably where he stood. She was starting to wonder what was wrong when she noticed the bulge in his pants.

A large bulge.

Maia froze in the water.

"Are your ribs still sore?" Calen asked.

She nodded.

"Then no."

He left without another word. Maia sank down in the water, but it was a mistake. She was too warm now. Hot enough to have to get out of the tub.

After that afternoon, Maia noticed Calen was aroused frequently.

They would be talking, catching each other up on their day, and she'd glance down to see his hard-on pressing against the front of his pants.

He never seemed embarrassed by it either. If he caught her noticing he'd just carry on with his side of the conversation as if nothing was different. Occasionally she thought she detected a hint of amusement in his eyes, but his features would remain impassive and non-threatening. She didn't get the sense he was laughing at her, or it would have been acutely uncomfortable.

Not that it was comfortable exactly. Though Calen was very controlled and never made a move on her, the air would fill with expectation—an expectation she wasn't brave enough to act upon yet. But she knew *he* would once she was healed. Maia couldn't believe Calen was so turned on by her, but she was trying to get used to the idea.

She now wore the loveliest clothes—beautiful flowing dresses that made the most of her slight curves. In reality, she didn't have much of a choice since Calen had gotten rid of her old wardrobe. But she had a hard time resenting him for it. The new clothes made her feel pretty. She loved them.

Maia was also wearing makeup for the first time. Not a lot of it, since she wasn't used to putting it on, but she learned to apply a touch of mascara and eye shadow as well as lip-gloss and a little powder. She had fun playing with it and silently acknowledged that it enhanced her features. When she looked in a mirror, she could almost believe she was good-looking enough for Calen. The illusion lasted only long enough for her to Google him again and compare herself to the women he'd been photographed with.

Not that Calen seemed to find her lacking, but she was suspicious of his appreciation. Given her situation, it was too convenient. She had the sneaking suspicion that the universe was laughing at her before it set her up for a big fall. Doom crept steadily closer.

Liam and Trick were fixtures at dinner, and they brought their sister Maggie with them whenever she was free. The friendly brunette was only a year older than her but already married. Maggie's husband was an FBI agent, of all things. They had met at a coffee shop and had dated for a year before tying the knot. Jason was by all accounts a friendly man whom Calen liked. But Jason didn't come over for dinner. Calen explained that it would create complications for him at work.

Though Calen continued to assure her he wasn't in the family business, Jason's superiors would have pressured him to surveil the McLachlans if he and Calen became too friendly. As it was, Jason had a self-imposed hands-off policy when it came to organized crime, preferring to work in white-collar crime and fraud. Maia thought that was wise.

Maggie wanted to organize a girl's night out with her and her best friend Peyton, but after one look at Calen's face, she declined. Apparently Maggie had not been told the whole truth about her. Maia put it off, making a vague promise to go out when she felt better.

Eventually, the day arrived for Maia to go back to work. She waited till her ankle was able to support her weight, although she used a cane for extra support. But it was getting better, and her ribs no longer hurt. There were only faint traces of her facial injuries left, too. Davis drove her to work on a Wednesday morning and assured her that Stephens was already there patrolling and checking the secure feeds from the cameras they had secretly installed. She felt guilty for not informing her coworkers about them, but it was better they not know.

Maia went inside and quickly greeted everyone. Everyone was excited to see her back. She was gratified by the concern over her 'accident', especially by her friends Chang and Wesley. They had dropped by her place when they found out she was hurt and were surprised to discover she had moved.

"Yeah, since I needed help, I sort of moved in with my boyfriend," she explained.

"Boyfriend?" Wesley asked quickly. "What boyfriend?"

"He's new," Maia said evasively.

"I guess that explains the new outfit. You dressing up for him?" Chang asked with a big grin.

Chang was the friendliest person in the lab and they often had lunch together. Maia glanced down at her fashionable dark grey wool dress and nodded sheepishly.

"Did he buy it for you?" he asked, noting the expensive cut curiously. Another nod. "He has good taste, you look incredible," Chang said, getting up to walk around her since Maia wasn't able to twirl for him just yet.

Wes frowned. "You moved in with some guy? Already? How long have you been dating?"

"Um, a little while. I met him during an outing with Tahlia," Maia lied, knowing that might distract him.

Wes was a fifth-year graduate student. He had asked Tahlia out after Maia had introduced them, but Tahlia hadn't been interested. Wes now avoided the other girl, so it wasn't likely her lie would be discovered.

"Oh," Wes said, pursing his lips. "You should tell him to swing by one day."

"When he's not busy, I'll ask him. I should go and check in with the boss now," she said, eagerly making her escape.

Out of the frying pan, into the fire.

Taking a deep breath, Maia walked to her boss's office and knocked on the pale grain wood door.

"Maia, it's so good to see you," Dr. Schroeder said as he rose from his office chair. His gaze dipped to her cane, and he added, "Sit, sit."

She took the seat opposite his desk and proceeded to catch him up on her condition and what research she'd been able to accomplish since they had seen each other last. When they were done updating and sharing news, she decided it was time to take her boss into their confidence.

Picking at the skirt of her dress nervously, she searched for the right words.

There aren't any. Just tell him.

"Boss, you grew up here in Boston, right?"

"Yes, why do you ask?" Dr. Schroeder said, leaning back in his chair with a puzzled smile.

He was a genial, fatherly sort of boss. She'd always felt lucky he was her advisor.

"Well, um, I thought I should warn you that you might have heard of my boyfriend," she said.

"You're not dating one of the Red Sox are you?" he asked, raising an eyebrow.

"No," she said softly. "His name is Calen McLachlan."

It was enough to wipe the smile from his face. "What? You're not serious are you? You have to break up with him!"

Maia winced. Calen had told her this would happen when he'd coached her on what to say the night before. *If they care about you at all, they'll tell you to stay away from me. Tell your boss enough of the truth to get him to leave it alone, but not enough to go to the police.*

"I can't," she said simply.

Her boss was quiet as he gave her injuries a second silent inventory.

"Maia what kind of trouble are you in?" he asked, his face tightening in concern.

"The big kind," she said honestly. "But he's not it. Calen is helping me, and the less you know, the better. I just needed to tell you because there will be people around because of me, and I didn't want you to be concerned."

"What kind of people?" he asked, looking slightly nauseated. "Criminals?"

"*No*. You don't have to worry about that. Calen stays away from his family's business. He is totally legitimate. But, because of who he is, he was in a position to help me. Now he's going to look after me."

"I see," Dr. Schroeder said slowly. "And these people you mentioned?"

"They're sort of bodyguard-type people. They'll be picking me up and dropping me off from work every day."

Her boss let out a shaky breath. "Jesus, Maia."

"Yeah, I know," she muttered, sinking farther in her chair.

"For how long is this going to go on? How long has this man said he's willing to look after you?"

"Um, a long time I think," she said meeting his eyes.

"What makes you say that?" he asked, his eyebrows pulling together.

"Because," Maia said, "he's going to marry me."

CHAPTER 13

*M*aia was glad when the day was over. She had a few experiments to catch up on, and getting around with her cane while getting them ready was tiring. Not as much as explaining her 'car accident', but almost as bad. When she was finished, she texted Davis on the new smartphone Calen had given her a few days ago and told him she was ready to leave.

Calen was now number one on her speed dial. Davis and Stephens were numbers two and three. As Davis had instructed, she didn't leave the building until the town car pulled up outside to wait for her. Stephens opened the door for her. She climbed inside and was startled to find she wasn't alone. Calen was sitting in the dark interior, talking on the phone.

"I thought we would stop somewhere for dinner to celebrate your first day back," he said, stopping his discussion to look at her.

She beamed, delighted to see him. "Sounds great."

His eyes were warm as he kissed her forehead before returning to his call. From his side of the conversation, she assumed he was talking to one of his alcohol distributors. Maia sat next to him silently, only half-listening as she took advantage of his distraction to study him without his awareness.

Then his hand drifted to her thigh while he spoke, stroking just under her hemline. When his fingers inched up, shifting her skirt up, she shot a nervous glance to the front seat where Davis was driving. Thankfully the privacy partition was up.

Calen didn't seem to realize what he was doing to her as the car crawled through rush hour traffic. His hand drifted up and down over her, baring more of her thigh to his touch. Heat pooled between her legs, and she squeezed them shut, trying to stop the sudden ache.

Embarrassed, Maia realized she was getting wet, but Calen didn't stop as he continued to haggle with his distributor. Then his hand shifted to caress her inner thigh. He was teasing her—intentionally.

Oh God.

Maia bit down on her lip as Calen's roving hand moved up to her panties, his fingers running over the cloth covering her already moist lips and sensitive clit. When his thumb pressed down on the hidden button, she couldn't suppress a whimper. Calen smiled and removed his hand for an instant to put a finger to his lips.

"Shh," he whispered before resuming his conversation.

Calen's fingers returned to her pussy, moving her panties aside so he could stroke her bare skin. Breathing faster, Maia clutched the fine leather of the seat under her hands. He ran his thumb over her clit in rough circular motion, making her suck in a ragged breath. His index finger began stroking her in earnest, rimming her entrance a few times until he pushed gently inside.

Maia gasped, her whole body tensing and shifting forward, unintentionally driving him deeper. She moved both her hands on top of his and then stopped, trying to decide whether to push his hands away or urge him closer.

CALEN'S ATTENTION was on Maia and her completely uninhibited response. She was trying to be quiet, but her breathing was audibly faster, and she kept shifting restlessly as he stroked her. She was so deliciously wet, but very tight around his finger. If he didn't know any better, he would guess that she was completely inexperienced.

He started to become sure of it when he added a second finger and his fairy flinched faintly. Calen hung up the phone without saying goodbye, dropping it next to him. Looking out the window, he checked their location. After making sure they were still far from the restaurant, he switched hands, stopping to taste her on his fingers before he put his arm around her to urge her closer.

Maia's eyes widened when she saw him lick his fingertips, but they had a glazed look to them that was deeply arousing. He was already hard as a rock, and she hadn't even touched him.

"Maia baby, how many lovers have you had?" he asked in a husky voice. She shook her head. "Is that a *no*, you don't want to tell me, or a *no* as in none?"

"None," she whispered in a breathy gasp as his thumb teased her clit more insistently.

Calen's expression turned predatory. "And no one has touched you like this before, with just a hand or a mouth?"

Again she shook her head, and satisfaction rushed through him.

"You were my first kiss the other night," she confessed in a whisper.

Calen froze in his tracks. Old fantasies flooded his mind and his cock twitched as his blood started pounding in his veins. It was like a switch had been flipped. He wasn't simply hungry for her now. Suddenly, he was ravenous. He wanted to be inside her this second, but her confession made that impossible. Later tonight was better—he would take Maia in his bed. She was almost completely healed. If he was gentle with her, he could move her into his room immediately.

The idea of sharing a room with Maia helped him take control of himself.

Calen focused on her again, circling and teasing until he was able to wring a loud gasp from her. He could feel the throb deep inside as her whole body clenched down on his hand. She bucked and gasped aloud before slumping back in the seat, her body hot and silky around his fingers.

Slowly he withdrew his hand, petting Maia gently over her panties as he waited for her to recover. When she couldn't catch her breath, he quickly wiped his hands on a handkerchief from the bar and put an arm around her shoulder, cuddling her closer to him.

Maia was still shivering from the aftershocks of her release. He felt each tremor deep in his groin. The impulse to take her home right now was strong. But he'd promised her a night out. And he was too hot for her right now. An evening out was a much better plan. It would give him some time to cool off.

He kissed Maia softly. "Okay now?"

She nodded yes this time, and he smiled. His fairy seemed to lose the power of speech when he touched her. Maia was usually so articulate, a detail he loved about her. But he might love her inability to speak right now a bit more, and her completely untrained response to his touch.

"So, I'm the first person to make you come?" he confirmed, looking down into her flushed face.

"Other than me you mean?" she replied, making him laugh.

"Yeah, other than you," he said with a grin.

"Yes," she whispered. "My first everything."

Pleased beyond measure, he leaned down to whisper in her ear. "I'm gonna want to see that sometime soon," he told her.

"See what?" she asked, confused.

"I want to see you touch yourself."

"Oh, God," Maia said blushing a rosier red.

She covered her face with her hands, and his hearty laugh filled the air.

CALEN HAD a way of making Maia feel like she was the only woman in the room. He completely ignored all the other women in the restaurant, despite the fact half of them gave him openly covetous looks. Even their waitress, a woman well into her forties, couldn't stop from flirting with him. It was enough to give a girl a complex.

The way he'd touched her in the car excited and unnerved her at the same time. In the dim light of the restaurant, she studied his sculpted cheekbones and soft, full lower lip. He caught her eye and she looked down at her plate bashfully.

I don't know if I can do this. She wasn't equipped to deal with this man. He was so handsome—not to mention blunt and aggressive. She could sense that about him, despite how he'd taken care of her. Nothing in her past experience, which was nil where men were concerned, had prepared her for someone like him.

But what choice did she have? Did she even want a choice? She was twenty-three now and still a virgin. Not by choice, either. More of a lack of opportunity...

Eventually, Calen's single-minded attention on her was enough to distract her from the eyes watching them, or rather watching him. He wanted to hear all about her day and on her boss's reaction to her news.

He questioned her closely, unsurprised by her boss's apparent dismay to her possible nuptials. "You think he's going to leave it alone? He won't do anything stupid like calling in the FBI, will he?"

"No, he promised as long as I wasn't doing anything—" she cut herself off, trying to decide how to explain her boss' concern.

"Anything what?" he asked, watching her through narrowed eyes.

"Anything against my will," she said finally with an apologetic shrug. "I assured him I wasn't, and he seemed okay with that."

Calen nodded in understanding. He didn't say anything else about it for the rest of dinner.

HE WAS STARTING to rethink his plan to seduce Maia that night. Her comment about not acting against her will was a dig to his conscience. If he rushed her into bed, he couldn't guarantee she would be doing it by choice, instead of giving in to what he wanted her to do.

Given Maia's inexperience, it would be easy to get her into bed. She would be putty in his hands. But he didn't want to compel her into it, or worse, have her give herself to him out of a sense of obligation. He did want her, but he wanted her willing, so hot for him she would combust. And he was pretty sure he would do the same. It had been touch and go there in the car. He had been ready to go up in flames just from watching her climax.

That kind of response was uncharacteristic of him. But he was quickly learning that living with a fairy meant things weren't going to be normal. And unless he wanted to lose his head completely, he needed to get a grip. Postponing until he was used to having Maia around would be better. However, he wasn't prepared to lose all the ground he had gained tonight.

When they returned to the penthouse he took her hand. "Maia I would like it if you moved into my room tonight."

She whirled around, shocked features colliding with his. Her little mouth was a round O. *So adorable.*

"Just to sleep," he assured her. "For now," he couldn't resist adding.

Maia closed her mouth. "Why just to sleep?" she asked slowly, surprising him.

He gave her a rueful grin, "Because you decided to go back to work this week. And what I have planned for you will take much more than one night."

"*Oh,*" Maia said, red staining her cheeks. "All right," she said finally. "I'll sleep in your room tonight."

"Good," he said softly before straightening and walking away with an easy stride.

"Where are you going?" she asked with a frown.

"To take a cold shower," he said, walking backwards to maintain eye contact.

Maia cocked her head at him, giving him a steady challenging look. "Okay, I'm going to go change."

WAS she trying to kill him?

Calen had put on boxer briefs after his cold shower, satisfied that he was in control. He wrapped a towel around his shoulders and walked into his bedroom to find Maia already in his bed—and all that bravado went out the window when he saw what she was wearing.

It was a short dusky blue nightgown—one he had picked out himself from photos his personal shopper had emailed him. He had made an excellent choice. The flowing gown made her eyes look bluer, and her skin shone like a pearl against it. Her orange-gold hair was loose around her shoulders, and she was watching him with a hint of a mischievous expression.

It was, to his knowledge, the first time she'd worn one of the nightgowns he'd given her. Why could she be wearing one of his old t-shirts again?

Calen silently acknowledged it wouldn't have made a difference. "You like to play with fire, nymph," he growled, dropping the towel as he climbed into bed next to her.

Her eyes were huge as she took in his bare chest. In response, it puffed out. He had never been prouder of his six-pack than he was at that moment. Hungry now, he reached for Maia and gave her a hard possessive kiss. With a feather light touch, he reached out and stroked the top of her décolletage with a brush of his finger, and she shivered.

Shit. He had intended on being noble and self-sacrificing tonight, but she was making it damn hard. Pun intended.

He'd no sooner touched the silky softness of her short nightgown than his instinct took over and he grabbed her and pulled her on top of him. Maia gave a little squeal before his lips met hers, and she shifted on top of him. With a herculean effort, he took one last taste and then bodily set her aside.

"Be good or prepare to lose every single one of your virginities right now," he growled.

"Every *single* one?" She giggled. "There's only one technically. Isn't there?"

He tweaked her nose and laughed. "So innocent. Unless there's something you want to tell me."

"No. At least I don't think so. Care to explain the third? Cause I think I know the second and no...I haven't done that either. You know that."

"Well," he said, running his hand down her body and over her pert little rear. He caressed the taught little cheeks and then ran his finger over the silky cloth over her rear entrance. "I would be most surprised if you weren't also a virgin here."

Maia turned beet red, blushing hotly over her face and chest as she pulled away. "Oh," she said, looking away.

The playful sexual tension in the air dissipated until it was just tension. Calen noticed the shift and took her chin in her hand until she looked up at him again.

"Hey, don't worry. I'm not really into that. I was joking." Maia frowned at him and he backtracked. "Okay, so not completely. I'm a little too into the idea of initiating you into everything but you don't have to do anything you don't want to do."

She nodded but still wouldn't look at him. "I don't know. Maybe it's nice. Sorry. I feel stupid now."

And he felt like crap. He nuzzled her hair. "Don't be embarrassed. I love your innocence."

"Mmmhh," Maia mumbled, avoiding his eyes.

"Mmh what?" Calen asked, tugging on a lock of her hair until she looked at him.

She sucked in a breath and then let it out. "What if that's *all* that you like about me? You do realize you can only take my virginity once right?"

He couldn't stop from chuckling. "Is that what you're worried about?"

Maia shifted uncomfortably. "Liam may have mentioned some-thing about your DVD collection," she said slowly.

Calen sat up. "What DVD collection?"

"Your collection. He mentioned that something in it might explain your interest in me. Why it is that you're willing to have me around..."

Maia lapsed into silence. She peeked at him from under her lashes, an uncertain look mixed with curiosity. It made him want to soothe her, and simultaneously pull her underneath him so he could have his wicked way with her.

"I see," he said eventually, trying very hard not to laugh.

Damn Liam and his big mouth.

MAIA WATCHED CALEN QUIETLY. His mouth was twisting and quirking like he was fighting a smile. The anxiety she had been experiencing started to fade, but her confusion was growing. What was so funny?

Eventually Calen snorted a little and got up off the bed. "Come with me," he said, extending a hand.

She stared at it, lips pursed before reaching out and using it to lever herself up. He shifted his hand to cup her backside to guide her out of the bedroom.

"Where are we going?"

"You'll see."

They made their way through the marbled hallway on bare feet. It should have been cold, but Calen had explained that the stones were heated by coils underneath the floor. When he bypassed the living room and the shelves of DVDs and Blue-ray disks, she shot him a questioning look, but he merely shook his head and led her to his office, flipping on the lights as he went.

"Over here," he said moving to the desk.

Maia looked around the room. There was no flat screen in here. Did he only watch porn on his laptop? Mentally fortifying herself she stepped around the desk to face the screen.

"Turn around nymph," Calen said, a little flatly.

She spun on her heel to face the shelf of leather-bound books behind her. He was running a hand over his face.

"What am I looking for?" she asked, her bewilderment clear in her tone.

Calen rubbed the back of his neck. "This is my collection," he said, gesturing to the books on the shelf behind the desk.

Her brow wrinkled. "What?"

"It's not a DVD collection. And I did not buy all of these. I did, however, buy a lot of them. Most of them. Only my closest friends know about this. A few of the brave bastards have even given some of these to me as gifts. It's not something I advertise to outsiders. Or to my family. In fact, I'm going to ask you to not mention this to your friends."

Maia looked at him with wide eyes and then at the volumes on the shelf. Most of the books looked old, like antiques. "Oh, sorry. When Liam said collection, I assumed it was DVDs. So, um, is this like vintage porn?" she asked.

Calen made a sound half-way between a cough and choking. "It's not a porn collection. Although if you ask Liam, he'd lie and say he caught me jacking off to a picture in one of these. I did *not* do that by the way," he said waving a finger in her face for emphasis. "He's a fucking liar, and you should never believe a word he says," he instructed as he pulled down a book with a bookmark sticking out of it.

Maia couldn't stifle a giggle as she took the book from him. She didn't believe him for a second. Flipping open the book to the page marked by the leather bookmark, her breath caught.

It was a stunning illustration of a fairy princess wearing a green and silver gown in a dark forest. The fairy had red-orange hair and blue-green eyes. Startled, she raised her eyes to Calen's face, but he wasn't looking at her. He was staring at the ceiling, and if she didn't know any better, she would have sworn he was blushing.

Maia set down the book and picked up another one with a bookmark sticking out of it. Another fey, a wood nymph with the same hair color was kneeling by a stream. She pulled down another book with a bookmark from the bookcase. This one was more elf than fairy, and she had brown hair, but her features looked similar to hers. Excited and blushing faintly, she scanned the other titles.

A Hystorie of the Fey and *The Fairie in England* were next to a leather bound volume of *A Midsummer Night's Dream*. A book called *Reflections on the The Cottingley Fairies* was the newest-looking book. Most of the others looked like antiques. She took down another one with a bookmark. Another fey look-alike with red-gold hair. Not feeling entirely steady, she sat down heavily in Calen's big leather desk chair.

She frowned at him. "Why don't the other women—the ones you were photographed with—why don't they look like this?"

Calen searched for the right answer. "I dated what was around me. And this," he gestured to the open books on his desk. "This isn't a thing for me. Or at least I didn't think it was until I saw you."

Heat coursed down her body, and she dropped her eyes to avoid the intensity of his gaze. A minute passed before she sneaked a look at him and found him still staring down at her.

"Well," she said finally before crossing her arms. "If it's not a thing, then why do you have all of these?" she asked, gesturing to the bookcase.

He shrugged. "I was always looking for elves and fairies in the garden when I was a little kid. I really believed in them. Not sure where it came from. I hadn't quite outgrown the phase when I started school. When I made friends with Liam, I made him go hunting fairies with me. Even at five years old that punk was humoring me. He didn't believe at all, but for my birthday that year, he stole this from the public library," he said, pointing to *The Fairy Catalogue*. The sticker with the Dewey decimal location was still on the spine. "And even though I grew up and no longer believe in fairies, I still buy these. Most of these volumes are antiques, Victorian era. Some are older than that. It's a hobby. One you are never ever allowed to tell anyone about."

Feeling wicked, Maia gave him a huge smile. But it must not have appeared as innocent as she intended because Calen crossed his arms and scowled a little.

"I'm serious about that," he said. "I will spank you if you ever breathe a word of it. I will probably spank you in any case because the mental images that suddenly crept into my head are just too good. Now...do you feel better or worse?"

Maia thought about it. "Better."

"About the spanking or about us?"

"About us," she laughed. "Although growing up looking like an elf was *torture*."

"I bet you were adorable."

"Not according to the boy in the third grade who pelted me with miniature candy canes," she huffed.

Putting an arm around her, Calen guided her back to the bedroom. "That boy was in love with you."

Maia scoffed. "His name was John, and he used to terrorize me."

"He was in love with you." His tone was superior and sure.

"He put glue in my hair and nearly blinded me with glitter!" she protested.

Calen froze. "What is his last name? I will find him and kick his ass," he said, stopping short and growling.

Maia ducked her head, a warm fuzzy feeling growing in the pit of her stomach. "I'm not going to tell you now." She laughed.

But it was nice knowing he was protective of her. No one had ever defended her before. And except for her mother, no one had ever tried to take care of her.

"You will tell me, or I *will* spank you," he said seriously.

Maia grinned at him and then threw herself into his arms. Looking surprised but pleased, he held her close against him before letting her go.

"We need to go to bed now," he said regretfully.

She nodded and they went back to the bedroom. Slipping into bed, she pulled up the covers to her chin. Calen drew them up to his waist, leaving his impressive chest in view. But she wasn't as intimidated by it anymore. In fact, for the first time, she felt almost comfortable around him.

CHAPTER 14

$\mathcal{T}$imur slammed his fist against the door of the bathroom stall over and over again until the metal was bent and smeared with blood.

That bitch was supposed to be his! For what she had seen, she wasn't allowed any other future. He was supposed to be the one fucking her, marking her. He had been eager to carve his name on that pristine white skin. It had been so soft, the perfect canvas. The girl would have begged him, pleaded for her life with those big jewel eyes. She wouldn't have lasted long, but their short time together would have been satisfying.

Then that fucking asshole McLachlan had shown up and demanded her as payment. And that shit Peter had let him take her. That moron, who his father admired so much for his brains, had agreed. After she'd seen him and Viktor in the woods with the body, that should have been impossible. But he'd always known Peter had it out for him. It wasn't enough that he was his father's right arm. No, Peter wanted to humiliate him, to make him live with the uncertainty of knowing there was a witness out there who could lock him away for the rest of his life.

For now, dealing with Peter would have to wait. He was already in trouble with his father for killing that *ublyudok* Oleg in the first place. But that little shit Oleg had talked back to him, and Timur had to show everyone that no one disrespected him. He was a Komarov. Oleg had just been some whore's son. Completely unimportant.

But his father didn't see it that way. That was why he'd been saddled with Viktor, his fucking minder. He'd told his father he didn't need a babysitter, but his protests had been ignored. Now he couldn't go anywhere without that hulking beast shadowing him. Except for today. He'd outsmarted him today.

Viktor had no idea he'd gone to the Harvard campus today to look for the girl. Even with Peter whispering poison in his father's ear, Timur still had loyal followers among his family's men. They'd been watching for him.

That fucking Mic had kept the girl close to him. Much closer than he'd expected. He'd thought McLachlan would keep the girl for a few days, tops. Maybe clean her up and send her on her way. He knew the guys reputation.

Calen McLachlan stayed out of the action, ran a lot of nightclubs. Was supposedly clean. Taking the girl had been a momentary impulse, a chance to be a hero. Timur knew he would lose interest. Then the girl would be up for grabs.

He knew her name and where she worked. His guys had even found out where she lived. It was only a matter of time before he would be able to pick her up again. Only McLachlan had moved her out of her shabby little apartment. At first, he'd thought he'd set her up somewhere new, but they couldn't find out where.

Until today.

Word had come early that the girl had shown up at her work. So he'd had Viktor take him out to one of his regular girls in the afternoon and then, after warning the whore to keep her mouth shut, he'd gone out the window. A cab ride later, and he'd been waiting inside one of the school's public buildings. One that had a view of the entrance to the building where the girl worked.

Snatching her in broad daylight wasn't his plan. He was too smart for that. No, he was only doing recon today. It had been so fucking boring. But his patience had been rewarded. Near six o'clock, the girl had left the building out the front door.

And she hadn't been alone. A bodyguard, a fucker as big as Viktor, had been with her. He'd walked her to an expensive town car, where another bodyguard had opened the door after stopping to talk to someone in the backseat. That was when he knew. McLachlan was there, in the car, waiting for her.

He'd been right about one thing. McLachlan had cleaned her up. New clothes and fine leather boots. With her hair and those eyes, she looked like a million bucks. A very high-priced whore.

Timur left the stall and ran his hand under the sink. Blood turned pick as it ran down the drain. He had to make himself presentable. His father was waiting, and no one kept the head of the family waiting.

He ran a hand through his hair and snorted. *The fucking Mic hadn't lied.* He was going to keep her. It should have never happened. The fact the bitch was walking around was an insult to him—an insult to his family. He was going to have to do something about that.

CHAPTER 15

Friday morning, Maia woke up in a panic. A huge weight was holding her down. She twisted slightly and realized the weight was Calen. His huge muscled upper body was partially wrapped around her and partly on top of her. And he was crushing her.

Suppressing her sigh, Maia looked up at the ceiling. She wanted to laugh, but Calen had come back late the night before. He'd gone to his club and had returned well after she had gone to bed. He'd woken her for a second when he slipped into bed, but he'd soothed her gently and told her to go back to sleep. She didn't want to wake him now, but she was starting to feel like a Cirque de Soleil contortionist as she wriggled and twisted to get out of bed. Throughout the whole thing, he stayed fast asleep.

When she was finally standing, she stopped to stare down at Calen's sleeping form.

His sculpted torso was turned on his side. Both his abs and muscled back were visible, the sheet tangled around his waist with one foot peeking out from underneath it. Maia took a deep breath. Calen belonged on the cover of a fitness magazine. And he was apparently a sound sleeper. He hadn't even stirred when she'd pried herself from under him.

Already dressed and ready to go, she heard a vibrating sound coming from the bed. Calen finally moved to press a button on his watch.

"Come here and kiss me goodbye, baby. I have a meeting, so I'll be a little late for dinner," he said in his early morning growl.

Trying not to betray her eagerness, she went over to him. He kissed her softly before dropping down and immediately falling back asleep.

Curious, she leaned over to examine the face of his watch before breaking out into a grin. Calen had set an alarm to kiss her goodbye. She went to work hugging that detail to herself.

"WHAT ARE you so keyed up about?" Wesley asked Maia near quitting time.

Startled, she glanced up from her computer. She'd been staring at it for a while without actually seeing it. "Hmm. What?"

"Are you okay?" Wes asked, watching her intently. "You seem tense."

"Oh, I'm fine," she lied as she packed up her new computer.

Calen had told her tonight was going to be special. He didn't need to spell it out for her. Tonight she was going to lose her virginity, and she had been trying all day not to think about it. She had failed spectacularly, vacillating between hot steamy fantasies and stomach twisting anxiety.

Maia knew she didn't have to do it. Calen had made that clear. If she didn't want to become intimate with him, they would figure something else out. But after he showed her his collection, that wasn't something she was willing to consider. Calen was her chance for a real life—a complete one with companionship, sex, and possibly even children.

But not love. That would be asking for too much.

Although, if she was honest with herself, she'd never expected that from her life. Love was something that happened to other people. People who weren't shy and introverted—girls like Tahlia and Maggie. Living without love wasn't going to kill her. It was just something she had to accept.

With all of those thoughts roiling through her mind, it was no wonder that Wes had noticed her distraction and anxiety. Everyone probably had. She wasn't good at hiding her emotions.

She was almost at the door when he stopped her with a hand on her shoulder. "Maia, if things are not going well with that new boyfriend, you should break up with him."

Where had that come from? "What? No. Everything is good. It's a big night is all. Date night," she added with a little blush.

"Are you sure that's all it is?" he asked, narrowing his eyes. "Because you've been different since you started seeing him. You wear different clothes and make-up. You get driven around in fancy cars. I think it's changing you."

Maia didn't know what to make of that. What he said was true, but it wasn't like she had a problem with those things. Or at least not a big one. Wearing the fancy clothes and makeup was still a novelty. She knew she looked different, but she loved all of her beautiful new clothes. Maybe that was shallow of her, but she had much bigger issues to worry about. Like sleeping with a man way too hot for her, or possibly being assassinated by Russians. She didn't need to add to the list.

"Maybe it might be, but I don't have a problem with that. Don't get me wrong, I appreciate your concern, but I'm happy with Calen. So please don't worry."

Wesley leaned in suddenly, crowding her a little. He put his hands on her shoulders. "You're so young and naive. I hate to see you get with some rich guy who just wants to control you."

Self-conscious now, Maia shrugged off his hands. "He's not like that," she said, uncomfortably aware she was lying.

Calen probably did want to control *someone*. She strongly

suspected he had been itching to explore that kind of a relationship for a while. And she had fallen into his lap.

"Have a good night," Maia said hastily, ducking under his arm and rushing out to Davis and the car.

On the way home, she shook off her encounter with Wes. She might have some misgivings about getting involved with Calen, but losing herself wasn't one of them. She might change a little, but she had lived a small and constricted life before that day in the woods. Calen was offering to show her a completely different world. Their relationship might not work out in the end, but right now she was finally living her life to the fullest. Whatever happened after, at least she would have some exciting memories to look back on.

Please let them be exciting and not terrifying.

She knew Calen would wait to become intimate if she asked. But living with him day in and day out had worn away whatever resistance she had. It had sparked a hunger inside her that was new and powerful. She wanted to touch him, be touched by him. She just hoped she didn't disappoint him.

At least he knew she was new at sex and wouldn't hold her inexperience against her.

Pushing away her apprehension and doubt, Maia decided to change into one of the silk dresses Calen had chosen for her. She rushed inside the penthouse and into the shower. Feeling decadent, she spent a good hour getting ready—shaving, primping, powdering, and brushing everything. When she was done, she took a long look at herself in the full-length mirror in Calen's room, admiring the effect.

Her eyes were lined with a smoky blue eyeliner, and her lips were rosy and full. The dusky blue dress she had chosen also made her eyes look like a darker blue. She was so flushed and overheated, she didn't bother with blush. Nervously, she fiddled with her hair, piling it up on her head loosely.

When she was done, she went to the living room to start a fire and wait for Calen to get home. As time went on, she grew more anxious. Deciding a little liquid courage might help, she made her way to the bar.

The amount of alcohol present rivaled the most well-stocked bars she'd ever been in. In the last of the early evening light, the bottles took on a glow, like so many liquid jewels. Some of these bottles were probably as expensive. Calen only liked the best.

Then why am I here?

Ruthlessly pushing that thought away, she poured herself a French cognac, sipping at it cautiously. She was tempted to pour Calen a whiskey, but she didn't know if it was like wine. Breathing was supposed to be good for wine, but whiskey? She would have to ask him later.

CALEN WAS in a foul temper when he got home. His day had been complete hell. The manager at Siren had caught one of the bartenders stealing credit card numbers from his patrons. Some of his customers had had thousands of dollars charged to their accounts unknowingly.

He'd spent the day making phone calls and putting out potential fires with exclusive offers and comped VIP packages to visit his other clubs in New York and Vegas. On top of that, one of his suppliers had crapped out on him and he'd had to find another on short notice. He had been fighting the impulse to put his fist through the wall for the last hour, but it all faded away into nothing when he arrived home to Maia.

A delicious smell filled the air as he stepped into the penthouse. But it was nowhere near as good as seeing his nymph kneeling in front of the fire in the living room waiting for him. She heard his steps and turned around to smile at him. Suddenly, it was the best day he'd ever had.

"Stay right there," she called to him as she rose and rushed to the bar.

His fairy was wearing one of her new dresses, a blue one. It floated around her svelte form and contrasted beautifully with her skin. Her hair was piled on her head in a loose bun, wavy tendrils escaping from it. It made him want to touch them.

She came back from the bar, extending a glass of his favorite whiskey. "I think this is the one you usually drink after work," she said, nodding to the glass.

"It is. You're very observant," he said, letting his muscles loosen as he took it from her.

Maia beamed. "I chose duck à l'orange for dinner tonight. I hope you like it," she said as he took the glass.

He stared at the whiskey before putting it down untouched. A drink was not what he needed. Instead, Calen pulled her into his arms, lifting her high against him. She squeaked slightly as his chest met hers, but he stopped the sound with his lips. Groaning aloud, he kissed her, pouring every ounce of need and passion he had into it. It seemed to go on forever, and was over way too soon.

"Thanks. I needed that, nymph," he whispered as he released her, sliding her down his body before setting her down on her feet. Maia swayed a little, and he held her closer until she stopped and turned those big extraordinary eyes on him. She stared up at his face until he stroked her cheek. "I hope you always look at me like that when I kiss you," he said softly.

"What?" she asked, still a little unsteady in his arms.

Calen laughed. He picked her up and hugged her till she squeaked again before he reluctantly let her go.

"Do you want to eat in the kitchen?" Maia asked, ducking her head before meeting his eyes.

She was feeling shyer than normal with him today, but that might have had something to do with the sexual tension sparking between them.

"No," he said, cocking his head and running his eyes down her body. She wasn't wearing any shoes, that perfect touch to his fantasy that a half-wild fey had somehow entered his apartment. "That dress deserves more than the kitchen bar. We'll eat in the dining room."

She helped him light candles, and he picked out an extra special bottle of red wine. Although she hadn't had a lot of wine before she'd met him, they'd already established that Maia like soft reds and sweet white wines. He opened his best Syrah and poured generous portions into cut crystal glasses.

He proceeded to ask Maia about her day. She shared the details bashfully, as if she thought they would bore him. But she was wrong. Hearing about her day, sharing her life, made him feel good.

Clean.

DESPITE THE DELICIOUSNESS of the meal, Maia could barely eat. She was so nervous and excited. Mostly nervous. She'd caught glimpses of Calen in various states of undress since she'd moved into his room. But she'd never seen him totally naked. She'd never seen any man without clothes, except on the Internet. And no one had ever seen her.

Maia didn't know how Calen was going to react when he saw her naked. Compared to the women he was used to sleeping with, she was a skinny twig with a boy's figure. In her anxiety, she started gulping her glass of wine, but after the second, Calen gently pried the glass from her hand and set it down resolutely.

"Thanks, baby. Dinner was perfect. I didn't think I could get in a good mood after the day I had," Calen said, leaning toward her to brush her hair away from her forehead.

"Hmm, I think Mrs. Portillo deserves most of the credit since she prepared the meal. I only threw it in the oven and followed her instructions. Why was your day bad?"

He told her about the problems he'd run into that day at the club. She listened sympathetically, and his shoulders eased. "It feels good to have someone to complain to," he said philosophically as he leaned back in his chair.

"It usually makes me feel better," Maia replied. "I know today sucked, but it must still be exciting to run your own club," she added, searching for something to cheer him up.

"It used to be. I never thought I would get sick of sitting at my own VIP table, watching people spend their money at *my* place. But it's gotten boring. The problems are all the same. I don't know. Maybe

I'm getting old, but being there now, forced to listen all the latest grinding music, is actual work now." He shrugged. "Liam wants me to open another club at the Caislean, but I can't bring myself to agree to it. I *should* do it. He is my best friend, and I owe him. But opening Siren Two isn't appealing right now."

"Yeah, I can see that." Maia nodded.

Calen pursed his lips and narrowed his eyes. "You didn't have a good time at the club at all, did you?"

"Sure I did," she protested. He gave her a knowing look, and she lowered her gaze. "Okay, it wasn't my idea of a good time. When Tahlia mentioned going there, I think I built it up in my mind too much. I was picturing something different."

"Different how?"

Maia shook her head ruefully. "Something old school and exclusive. Like a speakeasy. You know, softer music and a slightly dark ambiance. My mom used to dress like a flapper for Halloween, and I think I romanticized the whole prohibition-era culture," she said.

"Yeah, there's still a few speakeasies around as historical sites, but they're not opening a whole lot of new ones these days."

Maia smiled wistfully. "They should. They're just so...I don't know. They seem forbidden and secretive, but still fun and playful at the same time."

"When you put it that way, I guess it's too bad they went extinct," Calen said with a final bite of dinner. He put down his fork and studied her closely. "Why don't we have dessert in the living room in front of the fire?" he suggested, his pale blue eyes close to silver in the candlelight.

"Can I bring the wine?" she asked hopefully.

He shook his head. "I don't want you drunk," Calen said softly as he reached out to stroke her hair.

She shot him a brief faux scowl but couldn't hold it for long before she broke and laughed. He guided her to the living room and knelt to add logs to the fire before going back to the kitchen for their dessert.

"This is what I smelled when I walked in," he said, gesturing to the slices of peach pie she had chosen to go with the meal.

He had added a big scoop of vanilla bean ice cream to each plate. He handed one to Maia, and she took it eagerly. Eating dessert gave Maia something to do. She ended up demolishing it in record time, while Calen leisurely ate his, his legs stretched in front of the fire. Still feeling tipsy from the wine, she sidled closer to Calen on the couch. He put down his dish and moved his arm around her, cuddling her close. Maia's heart pounded as he caressed her neck and chin.

Cupping her face, he kissed her softly. "We can wait a little longer if you want, nymph. I mean not too much longer, because contrary to the impression I might have given, I don't actually enjoy cold showers," he said, making her giggle. "But if you don't want to do this tonight, we can wait."

Maia's heart was still pounding. She wanted to be with him. And it wasn't because she owed him so much. But she was confused about their relationship and what it was going to be like. He was holding back right now, she could tell, but what would happen when he stopped going easy on her?

Do you want him to take it easy on you?

What she really wanted was to live up to his expectations and then some. Impulsively, she slid out of Calen's grasp and down to the floor in front of him. She reached out and tentatively put her hands on his thighs, her eyes meeting his.

"I don't want to wait," she whispered.

CHAPTER 16

$\mathcal{C}$alen's blood flared hot when Maia went down on her knees. The unconscious gesture of submission was enough to drive him over the edge. He moved to follow her down to the floor, plunging his tongue into her mouth and covering her body with his. He slipped between her legs, making the silk material of the dress ride up along her thighs before running his hand over them. He gloried in his fairy's silky skin as he ground his hard length against her.

Maia was trembling slightly, but he didn't think it was from fear. No, her fast breathing and wide dilated eyes were proof of her sexual arousal. Her hands shook a little as she wrapped them around his neck. Pleased with her response, he pressed his erection against her, his hands caressing her bare legs and moving up to stroke between them. Her breath stuttered as he caressed the damp silk of her panties. He gave her a wicked grin before moving his mouth down her chin and neck, nibbling and licking until she was burning hot against him.

And then he stopped touching her. She whimpered aloud at the loss, her hands reaching for him as he pulled away. "It's okay, baby. I'll be right back," he said as he stood, pulling off his shirt as he went.

He walked to a closet and pulled out two fuzzy throws, almost identical to the one Maia loved to cuddle underneath in the living room except for the color. He'd thought they were useless and silly when his decorator had chosen them, but since Maia showed such a preference for them, he liked them now. He picked up the third and spread all of them in front of the fire. She watched him shyly, her skin deliciously flushed. Maintaining eye contact, he took off his pants and tossed them aside.

Maia's eyes flared when she saw his erection straining against his boxer briefs. He slipped them off slowly, and his hard length sprang free.

His fairy froze where she was sitting, like a deer in headlights. "I'm sorry. This isn't going to work," she said, slowly shaking her head.

His answering grin was predatory as he reached for her hand. He lifted her to her feet and then cupped her face in his hands.

"It's going to work just fine. Well, probably not at first," he added, honesty getting the better of him as he stopped to press a kiss on her forehead. "I'm going to fill you, and it will probably hurt in the beginning. But once you get used to it, you will feel good. I promise."

He waited until she nodded in assent, and then with a slow, deliberate movement, he took hold of the hem of her dress and pulled it up over her head. Embarrassed, Maia started to cover herself with her hands, but he held them still until she stopped trying.

"Let me see you," he coaxed as he held her away from him so he could admire her fully.

Maia was wearing a mint green lace demi-bra trimmed with black bows and matching panties. The color set off her hair and eyes and her skin almost glowed against it. She was breathtaking...and she was his.

He led his wide-eyed fairy to the blankets he'd used to make a nest in front of the fireplace. Following his lead, Maia knelt down on them. His blood was pounding in his ears as he followed her down, crawling over her until he was hovering just inches over her body. He couldn't remember the last time he'd been this excited.

Breathing in deeply, he inhaled her scent. Flowers. Maia smelled like flowers and sunshine. *How appropriate.* Lowering his arms, he covered her body with his.

Calen didn't waste any time. He slipped down the straps of that delicious little bra and unclipped it. He met her eyes before he removed it completely, waiting for permission. When she didn't move to stop him, he slid it away.

He stared at the perfect little confection before him. Her breasts were the same milky white as the rest of her, perfectly proportionate to her frame, but her nipples were a light brown. And they were already hard, like two toffee candies waiting for his attention.

"I'm sorry," Maia whispered.

Calen frowned. "Why?"

"They're too small," she said, moving her hands to cover her breasts.

He laughed aloud. "No, baby. They're perfect," he whispered huskily before kissing her softly on the lips briefly.

Maia didn't look convinced, but he did his best to distract her from her shyness and insecurity. To him, she *was* perfect. He loved the way her flush was working its way down from her face to her chest. Her eyes were squeezed shut, but they flew open when he trailed his hand down her throat and over her breasts.

His mouth followed the path his hand made. He kissed one perfect breast all around the nipple before taking the bud in his mouth and rolling his tongue over it. She gasped, and her body shifted restlessly underneath him.

Her movement teased his erection, making him want more. Eagerly, he parted her legs and moved between them, moving his naked length up and down over her cloth-covered pussy while he continued to kiss and suckle her nipples.

His little fairy was trying so hard to stifle her moans as he explored her body, but she couldn't. Pleased by all her little sounds, he replaced his lips on her breast with his hand.

"Kiss me hard, nymph," he whispered, before taking her mouth.

At first she was shy, meeting his stroking tongue tentatively, but after a minute her kiss became as heated as his as she tried to match his intensity. She broke off when his hands moved down to her panties and he started to push them down her body. He slid them off and moved down to cover the newly exposed area with his lips.

"Oh," Maia gasped as he kissed up the inside of her thigh to her pussy.

Deciding not to give her any time to recover, he pressed an open-mouthed kiss to her wet inner lips and licked up in a long stroke until he reached her clit. He nibbled and sucked the erect little nub until Maia was moaning and shifting under his hands, almost as if she was trying to wriggle away. But he wasn't letting her go anywhere now.

"Damn, you taste so good," he said in a tone of genuine appreciation as he rubbed his stubble against the soft skin of her inner thighs.

He moved back to her center, using his hands to part and stroke her lips as his tongue probed her small opening. He had to hold Maia still as he began to fuck her with his tongue.

"Oh, god, Calen!" Maia called out as she trembled and bucked under his mouth.

Amused, he paused to look up at her. "Am I going to have to tie you up, nymph?" he asked as he held her down a little more forcefully.

Maia's eyes widened, and she looked a little scared, but he could feel her getting wetter. Suddenly, he was excited about the idea of tying her up. It wasn't something he'd ever done with past lovers, not seriously anyway. He hadn't kept any of them around long enough to build up to something like that. But this fairy was his for keeps.

"We'll save that for later," he said, infusing his voice with command.

Maia shivered slightly.

Instead of feeling guilty, that shiver made him hornier. He didn't want Maia to be afraid of him, but having her look at him with that uncertainty in her eyes burned him up. Of course, if he ever did tie her up, there wouldn't be any doubt on her part. She would be sure of him, but for now, he did love watching her contemplate the unknown.

Maia was wild, almost dancing under his tongue as he held her down to keep her in place. He moved his hand up to join his mouth so his fingers could rub and circle her entrance. Sucking her clit into his mouth, he worked his finger inside of her. She was so tight her body resisted him, but he stroked carefully until he slid in and out easily.

He continued to work over her clit in his mouth before adding a second finger. Maia flinched a little as he slowly stretched her slick little sheath to be able to fit him. Clucking sympathetically, he used his tongue and lips to remove the sting. Soon she was moaning again, twisting slightly as he brought her closer and closer to orgasm. He could feel the telltale tremors start as her pussy walls started to clench and ripple around his fingers. Moving in rhythm with his hand, he sucked her clit harder until she gave an incoherent little scream, her pussy pulsing under his mouth and hand.

Maia went limp under him, but Calen didn't want to give her a chance to recover. She was still trying to catch her breath when he moved up her body. He wiped the excess moisture from around his mouth and then kissed her softly as he pressed himself against her tight wet opening.

"Hold on to me, nymph," he whispered into Maia's ear as he slowly and carefully began to push inside her.

MAIA GASPED when she felt Calen's rock-hard erection began to press into her core. Her hands clutched at his broad shoulders as he moved steadily inside of her. But it stung and burned as he parted her flesh with his own. Despite how wet she was—and despite an effort to suppress it—a whimper escaped. There was a momentary respite when he retreated, and she relaxed slightly.

"Just hold on nymph, the worst will be over soon," Calen said as he took hold of her hips and pushed slowly inside her before retreating.

He repeated the motion, working himself slightly deeper each time. Maia bit back a cry as tears filled her eyes. Acting on instinct, she stiffened as he moved forward.

"Don't tense up," he whispered into her hair, but she couldn't help it. She cringed, her entire body frozen underneath him. "Baby try to relax. It will start to feel better in a little bit," he said in a soothing tone.

Maia focused on his words and tried to follow his advice. "All right," she said, a little miserably, holding as still as possible while trying to relax.

Calen levered himself up on his hands to watch her face. "I didn't say stop breathing, baby."

Maia let out a pent up breath and laughed a little. She had been holding it unconsciously. "I didn't think it would be that bad," she said honestly.

"I'm sorry. I'm going to stay still until it doesn't hurt, okay?" Calen said softly, his voice a little strained as he bent to kiss her brow.

"Okay," she agreed, trying to catalogue the sensations in her as she looked into his silver-blue eyes.

For a split second, it had felt like he was tearing her apart, but the sting was already starting to fade, and she was getting restless, like she wanted to move. Tentatively, she flexed her muscles around his cock, rocking in exploration. Above her, Calen groaned and shifted. The pain returned, but it wasn't as sharp. Instead of flinching, she squeezed his arms tighter.

"Are you okay, nymph?" he asked hoarsely.

She waited. "I think so," she whispered when it was finally true.

The sting had faded again and the pleasure was slowly building. Tentatively, she flexed and rocked again until he let out a hiss.

CALEN SUSPECTED that his fairy was lying a little, but when she started moving, his hunger got the best of him and he was no longer capable of being noble. As carefully as he could, he began to move, pumping slowly in and out of her.

Being inside Maia was like nothing he had ever felt. Even now, it felt like her body was fighting to keep him out. He looked down, eager to see himself claiming his fairy. His gut seized a little when he saw a little blood, the proof of her innocence. It made him feel doubly guilty...but also crazy to fuck her harder, to imprint himself on her permanently.

He didn't, choosing instead a slow, easy pace to make sure he didn't hurt her. But he was intensely pleased. Maia truly belonged to him now, and no one else. He moved closer so she wouldn't see the blood, covering her like a blanket with just enough room at his hips to move back and forth.

Maia started to rock with him a little. The minute shift threw his gears into overload. "Shit, baby you're so tight," he panted as he increased his thrusts.

Maia whimpered again, but it sounded more like pleasure than pain this time. Which was good. He was trying to keep himself in check, moving gently inside her, but the need to pound into her was starting to overwhelm him. Incrementally, he sped up some more.

It wasn't going to take much more to come. Maia held him so firmly it was as if she was trying to strangle his cock, a pleasure close to pain. Her whimpers turned to breathy little moans, and he was finally sure she wasn't hurting anymore.

"Your cunt is so hot and sweet around my cock, baby. It's the wettest, tightest, best fucking thing I've ever felt," he whispered, panting the dirty words directly in her ear as he moved his hand between their bodies to stroke and squeeze her clit.

When his hand made contact, Maia gasped, and her little sheath tightened around him involuntarily.

"That's it, nymph, squeeze your little cunt around me. Yeah, just like that, baby. *Fuck!*" he exclaimed when he felt her inner muscles grip him tighter.

He rubbed her harder, and Maia began to cry out as he stroked in and out of her faster and faster. Her inner muscles rippled as her climax was on her, and she squeezed and clamped down on his dick, her entire body seizing with a strangled gasp.

Unable to fight his own climax anymore, he came hard, shouting at the ceiling and spilling his hot seed in jerking spasms. He kept fucking her through it, working his cum as deep inside her as he possibly could. He wanted to flood her little womb, staking his claim as primitively as he could.

By giving her his baby.

CHAPTER 17

*M*aia came back to reality slowly. Calen was pressed against her, a heavy weight on her body that she welcomed this time. He'd collapsed after giving a loud shout and rocking into her hard one last time. She had wanted to shout, too, but when her first real orgasm rocked her body, she'd been unable to do more than hold onto to him and gasp.

Calen's was still big in her, but she could feel him starting to soften.

There is a man inside me.

This was crazy. The sensation of being filled was so strange and alien. Paradoxically, she wanted to clamp down, to hold him inside her as tightly as possible, even though it had hurt in the beginning. She felt a tight, ticklish sensation deep where they were joined and a part of her wanted to rub and twist all over him again.

Eventually, Calen's breathing calmed, and he turned his head to the side to look down at her face. He kissed her softly. "Are you okay, nymph? I know it hurt at first. I'm sorry. It won't as much next time," he promised.

"It's not bad. Just a little burn," she told him. He nodded and slowly slid out of her.

Maia let out another little gasp. Even soft, he filled her well, and the sensation of him moving out of her body was startling. Calen moved away from her and she looked back down at her naked body. Silently cataloging the minute differences, she sat up.

She was overly conscious of her soreness. It almost felt as if he was still inside her. Or a ghost of him. Flexing experimentally, she flushed as she realized part of him *was* still inside her.

*Wait...*Calen hadn't used any protection.

Did he think she was on the pill? No. He knew she wasn't. Was she supposed to have asked him to use something? Or was he already on the baby train?

Maia froze.

Of course he is, you idiot.

MAIA'S SILENCE made him feel terrible. She was looking down at herself, an almost forlorn expression on her face.

Shit. She'd seen the blood. There was more than he'd thought there would be. It must have looked scary to her. Parts of it were pink where it mixed with his semen. Calen stood up to get a warm moist towel. He rushed back and started to clean her up.

"Let me do that," Maia said, embarrassed.

She took the towel from him and wiped away their fluids, wincing slightly when she touched a tender spot. Calen sat on the floor with his back to the front of the couch. He watched silently until she was done.

"Come here, baby," he gestured, one arm extended so he could put it around her.

Maia crawled next to him but sat a little farther away, outside of his embrace. She breathed in deeply and stared at the fire instead of looking at him.

"What's wrong?" he asked. Her lips parted, but she didn't answer, and he started to mentally swear. "I know it may have been rough. I meant to be gentle, but you're so small. It won't be so bad next time," he repeated apologetically.

She turned to him and gave him a wan smile that faded quickly. "It's not that. I mean it hurt, but I don't think it could have gone better. It was very nice at the end," she said with a slight blush.

"Then what's bothering you?"

Maia pulled her legs in against her chest and put her head down against her knees.

"This is not a trial period, is it?" she whispered.

"What do you mean?" he asked, confused.

"This is not a trial period if you don't use protection and I get pregnant right away. Is it?" she asked, finally looking at him. "Unless you forgot. Did you forget?"

Calen opened his mouth, but nothing came out. He wanted to reassure her, but there wasn't anything he could say. It was true. He'd never intended on letting her go...but fuck, if that's what she wanted he didn't have a choice. He couldn't force her to stay.

He sucked in a hard breath, bracing himself. "No. You're right. You don't get to choose. Not unless you want to run. I mean, you're probably not going to get pregnant after one time. We can call this all off right now, and you can leave tonight. If that's what you want, I will help you," he said softly.

Maia shook her head quickly. "I don't want to leave," she said before meeting his eyes with a frown. "As for tonight, not using protection—I should have asked before we did it. It's not fair blindsiding you like this. You assumed one thing, and I assumed another."

Calen put his arm around her. "Maia, I would never hurt you. What I want is to take care of you. I think we can have a good life together. A happy life. We can start using protection from now on if you are genuinely against having kids right away. But you did say you loved babies."

A corner of her mouth quirked up. "You have an excellent memory," she muttered.

"When it's something I like to hear, yes," he said, grinning unrepentantly before sobering. "But I can't guarantee my family's protection unless they think you're important to me. We are not always on the best of terms. I can handle my dad well enough these days, and it might take a long while for him to come around about you. He didn't want me to intervene the way I did. Colman's a stubborn old goat, and I don't like the idea of you having to live with any uncertainty until he does. And he's not even the biggest problem. His second, my cousin Darren, is the real issue. He hates me. But if you were pregnant, Darren would get on board, or it would look bad. Everyone would back you then. And," he added honestly, "I want kids. With you."

———

MAIA FELT like there was a bright spotlight shining on her. She'd been hoping to put off this talk about the future until later. Much later. But she'd been living on borrowed time from the start, and now she was out of it, too. She stared at Calen.

"Why me?"

He toyed with a stray lock of hair. "I think you're beautiful and funny and smart. And yeah, you look like jailbait and probably always will. That innocent look really does it for me."

Unable to help it, she laughed. "Okay. I think you're crazy, but I believe you mean what you say."

"Does that mean you're willing to getting married next Saturday?" he asked her.

She sucked in a breath. "Now I *know* you're crazy," she said shakily.

"It's for the best, nymph," he said, kissing the top of her head.

"I know," she said. "But it's so soon."

"It's not soon enough for me. And it doesn't have to be a big thing. A quick ceremony to make it legal. Then no one can touch you. Well... except for me."

Maia swallowed hard, but she nodded. "All right," she said, but she was still unsure, and it was probably obvious in her voice.

"What about the other thing?" he asked quietly.

A feeling of light-headedness swamped her. "A baby," she whispered.

He nodded, not bothering to remind her again that she loved babies. *Smart of him.* But Calen was extremely intelligent. Not to mention ruthless. He was also kind and generous...and too sexy for her piece of mind. And if she used the way he took care of her as an indication of how he would care for their child, he would be a wonderful father. Overprotective, but wonderful.

It wasn't politically correct for her to admit, but she wanted to give him what he wanted. It was instinctive, like breathing. Did that make her a submissive? Except for her, every woman in her department had read that Fifty Shades book. There had been endless discussion at coffee hour about it. Maia hadn't paid much attention at the time, but what if deep down she was *that* kind of woman? Should she be concerned about that?

She had always been shy, but she had always thought of herself as an independent person. And now the first man in her life was blowing up all of her preconceptions of herself. What if she wasn't who she'd always thought she was?

A tightness in her chest that she hadn't realized was there eased away slowly. So what if she wasn't? Should that stop her from seizing this chance? *Even if things don't work out afterwards, you'll never be alone if you have his baby.*

"Why don't we let nature take its course," she eventually agreed, taking a long look at Calen's long muscular body.

He was so damn masculine—his body screamed virile potent male strength. She'd probably be pregnant by the end of the month.

IMMENSELY SATISFIED, Calen wrapped his arms around Maia before dropping a kiss on her forehead. "We can get married here. Or at the Caislean. In fact, that would be a better place. I'll ask the guys and their sister. Some of my staff. And I should ask my father."

"Oh," Maia said. "Should I ask my coworkers?"

Calen relaxed. She wasn't going to change her mind or try to talk him out of it.

"Maybe just that girlfriend you mentioned. And your boss since he already knows. Is there anyone else you would want?"

"Chang and Wesley. They're my best friends in the lab. Well, Chang is my best friend, but I can't invite one without the other or I'd never hear the end of it from Wes." She smiled suddenly. "This is probably how wedding guest lists explode to unreasonable proportions."

He chuckled. "All right. They're going to find out anyway once the deed is done. You can shop for a wedding dress early next week. Why don't you ask Maggie and your friend to help you pick one out?"

"O-kay," she said, drawing out the syllables. "So I guess we are getting married next Saturday."

"Yes," Calen agreed, satisfaction dripping from the word like honey.

He squeezed her to him and pulled her into his lap. Despite the nagging guilt he felt, he was also aware of a deep sense of gratification. Determinedly, he pushed away the lingering remorse with the solid conviction that he was doing what was best for Maia, in both the short and the long term.

"You know, I think you were entirely too quiet when you climaxed," he murmured while kissing her ear and neck. "I take that personally. The next time you come, I'm going to make sure you're screaming my name."

And she did. Twice.

CHAPTER 18

aia was asleep, nestled in his arms late on Saturday morning when Calen received a call from Davis. Annoyed, he got up and went to the living room before the buzzing woke her up.

"What is it? Is something wrong?" he asked.

He was planning on calling Liam and Trick later to tell them the good news, but for the moment, he was happy to have time alone with Maia. Interruptions for anything short of an emergency were not going to go down well with him.

"Sorry, boss," Davis said, picking up on his tone immediately. "But there's some kid here looking for Maia, says he works with her."

"Really?" Calen asked suspiciously.

Maia wouldn't have told her coworkers her new address. She would have run it by him first. And he'd had her change all of her correspondence to a P.O. Box that Davis and Stephens checked for her. They brought her mail back to the penthouse and the bills for her cellphone came directly to him.

If this 'coworker' knew where Maia lived, it wasn't because she told him, nor did he simply see her new address on an envelope on her desk at work. He was either a spy from the Russians, or he had followed Maia home. Either way, he wasn't getting anywhere near her.

"Take him to the security office," he growled into the phone. "I'll be right there."

He walked back into the bedroom and threw on some clothes. Maia was still sleeping soundly when he left, but she hadn't gotten much sleep last night, so it wasn't surprising she was still out. He hadn't gotten a lot of sleep, either, but he was more accustomed to going without. And, in this case, it had been worth it.

Completely, amazingly worth it, he thought, replaying in his head giving Maia a bath, and then getting her all dirty again.

Calen walked into the security office, still buttoning his shirt. The kid was sitting in a chair surrounded by beefy-looking security personnel, his own and those that worked for the building. The intruder was young and clean-shaven, handsome enough, if you liked skinny and pale.

When the kid saw him, he sat back and gave him an obvious once over. His face tightened. Although he tried to hide it, a tremor in his hand betrayed his anxiety. He was also angry and resentful as he took in Calen's just-out-of-bed look.

Well, that explains his presence here. The little prick had a thing for Maia.

"So which one are you? Wesley, I assume. You don't look like a Chang," he drawled as he folded his arms and leaned on the wall across from the kid.

"Yeah, I'm Wes. Where's Maia? I want to see her," he asked, disdain in his voice.

Behind him, Davis lifted a brow, and Calen smirked back at him. The situation was becoming clear. The kid was here to warn Maia off of him.

"She's asleep. We were up late, and I'm not going to wake her. She needs her rest," he said, not pulling any punches. His tone and delivery made their late night activities clear. "Why are you here, bothering her on a weekend? What is so important that it couldn't wait till Monday?"

"I need to talk to her, and I want to see her now," Wes demanded.

If it wasn't for the petulance in his voice, Calen might actually respect the little prick. Instead, he was just annoyed—and getting closer to losing his temper.

"That's not going to happen. How did you get this address?" he asked, giving the kid his most steely expression, the one that had made the Russian's deal and his distributors and staff sweat bullets.

The kid shifted uncomfortably. "I got it from my cousin. He's a cop. Your address is not a secret," he said, his voice close to cracking.

No, it wasn't, but it also wasn't commonly known. Unless you were law enforcement.

"Let me guess. Your boss told you whom Maia is seeing and you want to rescue her from the evil mobster's son," he said, towering over the kid.

The irony of the situation wasn't lost on him. Under normal circumstances Maia and this kid would have ended up together. They would have had coffee break dates and gone out to movies. She probably would have ended up marrying him, or someone just like him.

Well, fuck that.

"That is not going to happen," he continued. "Maia is mine. She's marrying me. Next week, in fact. Your little crush on her is cute, but you are her coworker and nothing else. If I ever suspect you put your hands on my property, you will be in for a world of hurt. Am I clear?"

"You're getting *married*? She agreed to that?" Wesley asked, growing even paler than his normal pasty shade of white.

"Yes, she did," Calen bit back. "So when she invites you to the wedding, do yourself a favor. Tell her you can't make it. You're going to be out of town. Do you understand?" he said towering over Wesley.

The kid clenched his jaw. He didn't reply, but Calen kept staring down at him until he looked away. "Show him out," he told Davis, ignoring the kid's renewed protests as Davis and one of the apartment's security guards hauled him to his feet and out the door.

He was going to have to talk to his nymph about Wes. If the kid gave her trouble, he would step in, but not until he had a reason. As much as it grated, it was probably best if he didn't mess with Maia's situation at work or all of her co-workers would probably align themselves against him. He had to watch him step there. Unless the little prick touched her. Then all bets were off.

Calen made his way back to his place. He checked on Maia, and after finding her still asleep, started to get breakfast ready. Humming lightly, he squeezed some oranges and put the juice in the fridge to cool before starting on the pancakes. He was cutting strawberries for garnish, about to load everything on a tray, when Maia poked her head out of the bedroom.

Since her nightgown was lying on the living room floor and her clothes were still in the guest room, she'd pulled on one of his dress shirts. It fell below her knees, covering most of her body—but it was still the sexiest thing he'd ever seen. And his body responded in record time.

"Hi," she said, blushing madly.

Last night's activities flashed in his mind's eye like an expensive porno on fast forward. Tamping down a surge of lust, Calen smiled at her while serving some pancakes on a plate.

"Hi, yourself. Did you sleep well?" he asked, setting the plate in front of her on the kitchen bar.

"Good. You know...eventually," she said, still red and avoiding his eyes as she hopped onto one of the two barstools.

"Thank you," she said politely before picking up a fork and starting on the pancakes. She rolled her eyes after the first bite. "Oh, wow. These are incredible," she murmured. "Why do these taste so good?"

"They're from scratch, not a mix," he said, leaning against the counter across from her as he ate his own pancakes. "When we were little, Liam and Trick's mom always made them from scratch. After you get used to them that way, you can't go back," he said pouring maple syrup on top of the butter he'd already spread over his serving.

"Did you spend a lot of time with their family when you were little?" she asked between bites.

"Yeah. The Tyler's practically adopted me in grade school. My mom passed away when I was four, and since my dad was so wrapped up with other matters, he encouraged me to spend most of my free time with them. It was probably the single biggest mistake he ever made, and the luckiest of mine."

She raised her brows in question, fork still in her mouth. "They quickly became the most important influence in my life—not him," he explained. "They were...just a completely normal family. They had a station wagon and a camper. Two point five kids and a dog."

Maia wrinkled her nose. "Point five?"

"We didn't think Maggie should get a whole point. We were all pretty obnoxiously anti-girl until puberty," he said, pleased when she laughed.

Noting her good mood, he figured it was as good a time as any to discuss this morning's intruder.

"We had a little visitor today before you woke up. That Wesley kid from your work. I didn't want to wake you, so I sent him away," he told her, pouring her more juice.

Maia frowned. "But he doesn't have this address. At least, he shouldn't."

"Apparently he had a little talk with your boss. And the illustrious doctor spilled the beans about exactly who your new boyfriend is. Wesley is your wannabe white knight. He got my address from a relative in the BPD. They keep tabs on me as a rule. He may become a problem if you don't shut him down."

"My white knight? He wants to save me? From *you*? That's ridiculous," she scoffed.

"Your boss must not have told him the whole story. Or he doesn't believe I'm helping you. That, and Wes has a crush on you. Has he been bothering you at work?"

The last question had an edge he couldn't seem to hold back.

"No, not like that. And he does not have a crush on me," Maia said, squirming in her chair.

She was a terrible liar. Calen would have been amused if the subject hadn't involved another man. Or, in this case, boy.

"Yes, he *does*. What did he do?" he demanded as he leaned on the counter with both hands.

THOUGH HIS VOICE was still mild, Calen's face had grown hard and cold. Maia was uneasy. Given what they had done last night, several times, the change in him was disconcerting.

Calen was her lover now, but he wasn't her friend and their relationship wasn't equal. She had better not forget that.

"He *doesn't* have a crush," she insisted. "And he didn't do anything except express concern about all the new clothes and bodyguards. And that you were expecting," she added.

Calen didn't look convinced. "If he so much as lays a finger on you, I will find out and take care of it," he said, a trace of warning in his tone.

Maia froze mid-bite. She swallowed a mouthful of pancake that was suddenly too big. Despite feeling daunted, she shook her head. She couldn't let him scare off her friends and coworkers. It would set a bad precedent. Whatever Wesley's problem was, she would take care of it herself.

"He's not going to do that. And even if he did, *I* would take care of it," she said, trying to sound firm.

However, her voice squeaked a little, and Calen let out a frustrated sigh.

"Baby, I'm not trying to intimidate *you*, but you're going to be my wife soon. Anyone who even thinks about laying a hand on my wife is going to get straightened out. *Hard.* And that kid is definitely into you. Probably more now that he thinks you're a damsel in distress."

Maia chose her words carefully. "I can see your point of view. It would not be okay if Wes made a pass at me—but he's not going to. Honestly! Wes likes my friend Tahlia. He asked her out, and she turned him down. He avoids her now, but if she wagged her little finger, he'd go running like that," she said, snapping her fingers.

Calen shook his head. "Maybe he was into this other girl, but he's over it. He likes you now. Trust me. But you, my sweet little nymph..." he said, coming around the bar, "...you belong to me." He picked her up out of her seat and carried her to the bedroom.

BY THE TIME Sunday night rolled around, Maia was aching and sore. She had had more sex in the last forty-eight hours than she'd ever thought possible. Calen was insatiable. His desire for her was intoxicating...and a bit exhausting.

Calen did his best to make her feel comfortable with the rapid change in their sex life. He talked to her before, during, and after lovemaking. He wanted to know everything about her, and he was pretty open about himself. Maia had learned a lot about him in the last few days.

His favorite meal was Beef Wellington, and his favorite drink was Scotch, although he preferred wine with dinner. His favorite color was forest green, and his favorite designer was Ozwald Boateng. Maia couldn't have named any designers on a bet.

Calen also confided in her. His clubs were doing well, but lately things had gotten repetitive, and he no longer found it a challenge. He told her about his only serious relationship—a high school girlfriend. She would have been jealous if he hadn't also told her that the woman was happily married now with three kids. He also told her travel stories and about adventures taken with his college friends.

Maia was fascinated by his life and wished she had exciting stories to share with him as well. However, he seemed more than satisfied with hearing about her childhood with a single mother and her quiet studious life.

"What about travel? Or family vacations?" he asked, stroking down her hip as she lay next to him in bed on Sunday evening.

"There were only a few trips. We didn't have much money, but my mom had a friend who owned this big dilapidated beach house on the Oregon coast. It was cold and drafty, but we would wear big thick sweaters and go outside to build bonfires on the beach. I loved going down there," she confessed.

"Have you ever been out of the U.S.?"

"No. Just here and Oregon. I have pictures from a trip to San Francisco that my mom took with a boyfriend once, but I was too little to remember it," she said, cuddling closer to him

Calen shifted to spoon against her. "I'm going to take you to all of the major capitals of the world. I want to pose you in front of famous monuments, like the garden gnome in *Amelie,* only cuter," he murmured, nuzzling her ear.

"You don't have to go out of your way," Maia said, turning to him. "Unless you like traveling," she added hopefully.

Laughing at her transparency, Calen assured he did before sitting up and getting out of bed.

"We need to eat something. Gotta keep our energy up so we can do this all over again," he said, tugging on Maia's arms.

Groaning, she stood up and threw a silk robe over her naked body. She followed him out to the kitchen where they raided the refrigerator and ate at the bar in the kitchen again instead of the cold formal dining room.

After dinner, he told her about the phone calls he'd made inviting his friends to their wedding.

They were sitting in front of the fire. Calen was surprisingly fond of cuddling.

"How shocked were they?" She grinned up at him from the circle of his arms.

"Liam and Trick were forewarned, so they weren't surprised. They said Maggie would be thrilled to come over and help you pick out a wedding dress. As for the rest of the guys, they *were* surprised. I think the fact I own nightclubs makes me seem like more of a player to them than I actually am. My friend Alex promised to make it over with his wife Elynn. They're newly married. You'll like her. She's a scientist of some kind, too. Sergei and Giancarlo are trying to clear their schedules, but Sergei will definitely make it. He knows I'll kick his ass if he doesn't. Next to Liam, he's my best friend. We spent most of our freshman year at University puking into each other's dorm room toilets."

"Sounds like a good way to bond." She giggled. "I don't think I've ever been drunk."

"*Really?* Now that is something that has to change. I wish I'd known that yesterday because now all I want is to see you drunk. You would be so cute buzzed. Now it's going to have to wait for our honeymoon, unless you want to nurse a hangover at work. I don't recommend that."

Her head swam a bit at the mention of a honeymoon. "Are we having one of those? A honeymoon? I just took so much time off, I don't think I can afford to take anymore so soon."

"Your boss will understand if you take a week off for your own honeymoon. If you need me to talk to him, I can give him a call tomorrow."

Maia hurriedly promised to do it herself. She didn't want Calen calling her boss and intimidating him. Dr. Schroeder probably wouldn't begrudge her the time off. In fact, he usually suggested she go home early every night. He seemed overly concerned about keeping Calen happy.

"Where will we go?" she asked.

"Where have you always wanted to travel?"

"I don't know. Everywhere. The Grand Canyon or the Florida Keys," she said earnestly.

He laughed. "I was thinking Europe. Like France or Italy. Wouldn't you want to see Paris or Rome?"

Maia's breath caught. He had promised to show her the world, but actually making plans was something else. It would be a dream come true to see Europe, one that had always seemed too far out of her reach unless she was able to go to a conference there. And, unfortunately, she hadn't gained enough seniority in the lab for that.

"Yes!" she said, jumping to her knees on the sofa and squeezing Calen with all her strength.

He hugged her back just as tightly. "Which city would please you best, nymph?" he asked, stroking her hair.

"Either, I don't care," she said excitedly.

"Then I think I want to do a little research and surprise you. If you genuinely have no strong preference, that is."

"A surprise would be nice," she whispered, cuddling closer to him.

Growing up, there hadn't been a lot of extra money for gifts at birthdays or Christmas. Maia had always known exactly what she was getting—clothes or shoes—whichever she needed the most at the time. She had always secretly hoped for more surprises during those occasions, but had been careful not to let her mother know. She never wanted her mom to think she'd been unhappy with what she'd received. It had been hard enough for Coleen O'Donnell Dahl to make ends meet.

Calen's eyes held a hint of sympathy, as if he could read her mind enough to know what surprises meant to her and why. And he probably did know. He had questioned her carefully on her life and childhood. In his eyes, her childhood had been bleak and deprived. Consequently, he seemed to revel in spoiling her.

"Then a surprise you'll get," he promised.

CHAPTER 19

*M*aia's announcement that she was getting married, and the invitations to the wedding, threw her little lab into an uproar. She went ahead and invited everyone since Calen had told her the Caislean's ballroom capacity was 500 people. They were technically only inviting a tenth of that.

She was nervous about Wesley's reaction, but he didn't say anything in front of the group. Relaxing she went about her work cheerfully. Calen had been overreacting. Wes was simply a concerned friend.

Later that afternoon, she went to the basement to get a bottle of industrial grade ethanol from the inflammables locker downstairs to finish her experiments. The basement was in fact a series of interconnected rooms and hallways, some of which were tunnels that connected to the adjoining buildings. She loved it down there. It was overflow storage for the Herbaria and the Museum of Comparative Zoology.

When she had first started work, she had gotten the grand tour of the place from one of the senior researchers in the lab. He had shown her the old bone casts of primordial human ancestors stored down here. The replica 'Lucy' specimen of *Australopithecus afarensis* was still periodically used by the human anthropology class for study. But that was only the start of the strange and mysterious objects that could be found in the basement.

Her favorite things were the drawers of mounted beetle specimens that shined like iridescent jewels. She'd been tempted to start collecting insects when she'd first seen them, but her place had been too small for a collection of any kind. Now that she lived in a huge penthouse, maybe she could start. Although, Calen would probably appreciate it more if she brought her work home and collected butterflies instead. Butterflies went with the fairy image a lot better.

Of course, not all the specimens and overflow displays were pleasant. The old stuffed marsupials were rather creepy. So were the taxidermy bird specimens. And the big waterproof crates that housed the old ichthyology specimens preserved in a dark blue inky substance were also pretty ghastly. Of course, that might be because she'd never been that fond of fish, except as sushi.

She was carrying the bottle of ethanol to the stairs when a sudden motion behind her almost startled her into dropping it.

"Jesus, Wes! You scared me half to death. Don't sneak up on me like that!" she admonished.

Wes stepped closer to her with a serious and determined expression. He put his hands on her shoulders and Maia's heart sank.

"Maia, you need to go to the police. My cousin is on the force. You don't have to marry that guy! I can help you," he said, trying to draw her into his arms.

She resisted his pull, trying to put the bottle between the two of them as a shield. "Let go, Wes. I'm not doing anything I don't want to do. I'm marrying Calen because I want to," she said.

"Maia, Doc Schroeder told me everything! I know you think you have to marry this guy, but you don't have to! The police can have him arrested for kidnapping and extortion or something."

"Calen is not a criminal, and he hasn't done any of those things. He's protecting me!"

"From his own family, I bet." Wesley's face was ugly. "And you're kidding yourself about him. I've met the guy—he just wants a sweet innocent girl to corrupt and use for his own sick fantasies. He's making you sleep with him, isn't he? He made that pretty fucking clear."

Maia pushed Wesley's restraining arm away with her shoulder. He was bigger than her, though, and he simply put them right back on her again. "Stop that!" she hissed. "And the danger is not from his family. Believe me when I say that. I can't tell you what happened, but Calen saved me. And he wants to marry me now and start a family. I'm very lucky."

Wes let out a disbelieving bark of laughter. "Oh, my god. I don't believe this. He's brainwashed you! Or is his dick that powerful? Has he fucked you into submission?"

Maia's face hardened, and she gripped the bottle harder to keep herself from slapping Wes in the face.

"You should mind your own fucking business!" she shouted, the hurt mingling with the anger in her voice.

Maia never used swear words, but she was so mad. Unfortunately, being so angry only made her want to cry instead. Shoving away the humiliated tears that were threatening to fall, she hugged the bottle to her chest defensively.

"Maia, I'm sorry," Wes said, immediately contrite. He tried to hug her again, but she shoved him away again. "But I'm worried about you. I care about you. Before this whole mess started, I was going to ask you out. I really like you. In fact, I more than like you. I love you."

Maia couldn't believe her ears. She also didn't believe him. Calen was right. Wes was suffering from white knight syndrome.

"*No, you don't.* A few weeks ago, you were in love with Tahlia. And I don't like you that way. I never have. You're just eager to come to the rescue—one that is completely unwarranted and unwanted. Calen and I are getting married and starting a family. I may be pregnant now, for all I know," she argued before shoving him out the way.

She left him gaping at her from the bottom of the stairs.

Maia ignored Wes for the rest of the day. Instead, she gossiped with Chang about her upcoming plans. Dr. Schroeder had, as Calen predicted, offered her time off for a honeymoon as soon as he received his invitation to the wedding. Though he seemed anxious for her, probably because Wes had gotten him worked up, her cheerful demeanor seemed to calm his fears enough for him to agree to attend the wedding.

She was so preoccupied with the day's events, she didn't notice Davis and Stephens' alert attitude and edgy behavior. They actually met her in her office when she texted that she was ready to leave, carrying her bag on the way out. Davis shot Wes a hard look before they left, but she chalked that up to his visit over the weekend.

Calen was waiting for her when she arrived home. He came right up to her and swept her into his arms, exchanging a nod over her head with Davis who departed with his usual stealth.

"What's wrong?" she asked.

He looked so serious and was holding her tightly. "I thought you might still be feeling bad about that scene with Wes," he said, sitting down in front of the fireplace with her on his lap.

Maia went rigid. Belatedly, she remembered the cameras. They had told her they were putting some in the basement. She had assumed they were putting them on the doors and entrances, but they must cover a wider area than she had supposed.

"*Oh.*" Of course they were watching. They couldn't protect her if they didn't. She had to remind herself that the cameras were going to see everything. Even what she didn't want them to see. "I'm okay. I guess you know?"

"Davis was monitoring the feeds, and he gave me a call. I saw the playback. I know you handled yourself well, but you were swearing and almost crying. I don't like that little shit upsetting you. I can talk to him if you want. In fact, I think I should."

"*No.* I told you I would handle it and I did. And I was more angry than anything. It's just that when I get real mad I want to cry instead," she said, letting out a huff.

"Remind me not to make you mad," Calen said, gently cupping her chin with his hand. "I don't ever want tears from you," he added as he kissed her forehead.

"It's not a trait I'm proud of," Maia grumbled. Tears were a weakness and she hated that they came so easily when she was upset. "When my mom was sick I was angry with lots of different people. The insurance company got an earful when they tried to cancel her health insurance. But it didn't help my cause that I kept bursting into tears during the negotiations. We kept her insurance, but they decreased her coverage so we had to pay more out of pocket. There were a couple of bitchy nurses that made me cry too when she was in the hospital. That never ended well."

"I'm sorry about that, nymph," he said, running a hand down her back. "I won't talk to Wes if you don't want me to. *If* he leaves you alone from now on. But one more little scene like that, and I will go down and have a talk with him personally."

Maia frowned, but she didn't think she was going to get a better offer from him. "Did you rush home early because of Wes?"

Calen shifted and held her a little closer. "Well, that was bad timing, but I also got a call from my Da today. I left him a message inviting him to the wedding, and he was calling me back."

"I see. How did he take it?" she asked uncertainly, drawing away from him to see his face more clearly.

"Never mind his reaction. If I don't mind his fine feelings, neither should you. It's what else he told me that you should know about."

"What is it?" Maia asked, growing anxious.

He put his hands on either side of his face. "Da said the Russians had been in touch. Apparently Timur has been giving his father a headache. Enough for them to make an offer. They want to negotiate."

Maia felt a cold chill pass through her. Stomach clenched, she took a painful breath. "What do they want to negotiate?"

"Your purchase. They want to buy you back."

Dizzy with fear and sick to her stomach, Maia covered her face with shaky hands. She knew what that was code for. They wanted her dead.

Calen squeezed her tight. "Don't worry, baby. They're not going to get their hands on you. I made sure Da knows that I am not giving you up, and he's going to drive that home to them. They'll back down. I promise you that."

Maia buried her head in his chest, trying not to panic. His father had probably tried to talk Calen into handing her over to the Russians. He wouldn't have wanted his son sticking his neck out for a stranger.

"Don't worry," he soothed while stroking her hair. "Just focus on our wedding plans. They won't bother us after we're married. In the meantime, I'm doubling your security detail. After the wedding, we can go back to four, but in the meantime, they're attached to you at the hip. We're going to send someone in as a janitor to your work this week, too. Once we're married, this 'offer' will disappear. But for now, the trip to the bridal store is out. A selection of dresses will be sent here tomorrow instead. Have you gotten ahold of Tahlia?"

Maia made an effort to get ahold of herself. This is why Calen was marrying her. She would be safe once they said their vows. "Yes, she's free tomorrow. So is Chang," she whispered tightly.

"The Asian boy from work?"

"Chinese, and yes."

"As long as it's not Wes, I guess that's okay. You can change in our room and come out here to model the dresses. I've taken the liberty of picking out a few in different styles for you to choose from, as well as others the dress coordinator will bring along based on your coloring and measurements. The club is sending over champagne and wine and Mrs. Portillo will fix some hors d'oeuvres."

That distracted her. She wondered what sort of dresses Calen would pick. Since Maia had never given wedding dresses a second thought, it didn't matter, as long as it fit and didn't make her look shorter than she was. She nodded weakly despite her continued anxiety.

Calen kissed her, and she burrowed against him, grateful for the feel of his strong arms around her.

Despite his assurances, she was tense for the rest of the night. The next day at work she was distracted, but her boss chalked it up to wedding excitement, and she let everyone believe that. At the end of the day, Chang joined her in the town car to Calen's penthouse where Tahlia was waiting in the lobby for them. Her friends both eyed each other over the bodyguards, but neither said anything as they went upstairs, chatting animatedly.

Mrs. Portillo was waiting for them with trays of tasty treats to nibble on. There was also chilled champagne and another sweet French wine from the Rivesalte region.

Tahlia and Chang have never hung out together, and they were having fun getting to know each other—although Tahlia was a little quieter than usual at first. But the lovely brunette seemed happy about Maia's impending marriage. A little surprised, but definitely pleased.

"Where is the groom-to-be?" Tahlia asked, sipping on champagne while admiring the kitchen and adjoining living room.

"Calen is going out with his friends for dinner. He's promised to stay away until at least eleven, so we'll have plenty of time to pick the dress and do the first fitting. His best friend's sister Maggie and her friend Peyton are coming over, too. He wants me to get to know them better since we'll be spending a lot of time with them in the future."

Tahlia's face lit up. "That's good. I've been thinking you needed to get out more and make new friends," she said, an odd light in her clear blue eyes.

"I've never met Peyton, but Maggie is nice. Her husband is an FBI agent."

Tahlia didn't even blink when she nodded, which suggested that she didn't know about Calen's family.

The two women in question soon joined them. Peyton was a very pretty girl with auburn hair. Watching her laugh at something Chang said, Maia wondered if Calen had spent any real time with Peyton before. She was pretty enough to have caught his eye. But Peyton didn't seem at all upset by the fact that Calen was getting married. She seemed perfectly genuine when she congratulated Maia.

After they had spent a little while eating and chatting, the dress coordinator arrived with a dozen gowns to choose from. Maia immediately knew which one Calen wanted her to wear, but she was so spoiled for choice that she decided to try them all on. The others encouraged her to do exactly that, and soon they were sitting on the long couch in front of the fireplace, sipping champagne and cheering her on as she twirled and modeled thousands of dollars worth of wedding finery.

There was one choice she saved for last, knowing that it was the one she would ultimately choose. She slipped the white silk confection on, and the dress coordinator helped her adjust the corset bodice to conform to her body.

The straight cut bodice lifted and molded her cleavage. It was overlaid with a gauzy embroidered white silk that matched the skirt, which floated around her legs in asymmetrical layers.

The coordinator tried to give her a matching coronet for her hair, but Maia drew the line at that. The dress already screamed fairy princess without it. Instead, she asked for white orchids to be put in her hair the day of the wedding and the coordinator promised to arrange it.

"So this is the one?" the eager woman asked.

"Yes, definitely," Maia said, running her hands over the delicate material reverently. "Is this one of the dresses my fiancé chose?"

The woman nodded, pins in her mouth. Satisfaction flooded Maia. This was the dress Calen wanted her to wear. She knew it instinctively. He still left the choice up to her, but this one was his fantasy. And it was beautiful.

Is this the way he really sees me? Maia ran a hand over the sudden flurry of butterflies in her stomach.

The dress lady said something, but her voice was distant and tinny.

"I'm sorry, what was that?"

"I said I agree," the woman said, adjusting the bodice, having taken the pins out of her mouth. "The others are lovely, but this one seems like it was made for you. I'm sure your audience out there will say the same thing. Go out and show them!"

When Maia did, the girls and Chang hooted and hollered louder than they had for any of the other dresses. It was a smashing success.

She pirouetted and twirled before announcing. "This is the dress I'm going to be married in. I think it suits me best, and I'm positive it's the one Calen wants me to wear. He didn't say so, but I think it's obvious."

"Yeah, it is. Man, he's not kidding around about the fairy fetish," a red-faced and tipsy Peyton giggled.

"Peyton," Maggie hissed, poking her in the side with an elbow.

"Oh, I'm sorry," Peyton said horrified, her hand flying to cover her mouth.

"A *what* fetish?" Tahlia asked with a grin.

The wine had loosened up her usual reserved demeanor and she was laughing and joking in a way Maia hadn't ever seen. Not even on her own birthday.

"I take it you know about Calen's collection," she said to Peyton before she could stop herself.

"Oh, thank god!" Peyton said, collapsing onto the couch in relief. "You know about his collection, too!"

Maggie smiled sheepishly. "Me and Liam have gone shopping for the collection together before...and I have a big mouth. But Calen doesn't know I know. Please don't tell him!"

"What collection?" Chang asked wide-eyed, bouncing up and down on the plush couch cushions in his excitement.

The glass of wine he was holding sloshed dangerously. Tahlia took it out of his hands before Maia answered.

"I'm not allowed to discuss Calen's collection," Maia said, trying hard not to laugh. "But I will say that I was relieved to find out it did not involve porn of any kind."

The girls burst into laughter, and Chang begged to be let in on the secret, but Maia was adamant. She had promised Calen. Peyton and Maggie could tell him in the elevator when they all went down if they chose. They had already offered to give him a ride home.

"And this is the man that owns all those nightclubs?" Tahlia asked. "Including Siren? He is starting to sound interesting. I wish I could meet him."

Tahlia had already announced she needed to leave early, before Calen arrived home. She also had a family event she couldn't get out of and wouldn't be able to attend the wedding that weekend.

"You'll meet him when you get back from Florida," Maia said.

Tahlia's smile stiffened, but she agreed. "Of course I will."

The coordinator's assistant came out of the bedroom after they finished packing the rejected gowns. She took some measurements and announced that the necessary alterations would be minimal and mostly to the hemline of her dress. Maia changed back into her clothes and started to celebrate with more wine.

Tahlia had already been gone for half an hour when Calen came home. He breezed in with Liam and Trick, all of them flushed and talking loudly. They swept into the room, filling it with their presence. The Tylers were impeccably dressed, as usual, but Calen put them to shame in his tailored charcoal grey suit.

The trio had clearly been drinking, too.

"Hello, nymph," he said, sweeping in and kissing Maia soundly.

The others snickered. Chang hopped up to say hello, his face flushed and excited. At first, Calen was guarded, but polite. But after some more chatting and a round of toasts made by Trick, Calen warmed up to her other office-mate. He even invited Chang to the bachelor party Liam had decided to throw him on Friday night.

Feeling festive, Maia joined Maggie and Peyton as they grew more and more tipsy. By the time everyone left, she was as drunk as she'd ever been. Soon the others got up to say their goodbyes. Chang left with the girls, thrilled to be included.

"I think you have a new fan," Maia said, carefully making her way to him on unsteady feet.

Calen watched her with a big grin. He cocked his head at her.

"Baby, are you drunk?"

"I'm definitely not sober." She giggled as she reached for him.

He let out a little growl as he reached for her. "I think this calls for some nakedness," he murmured in her ear as he carried her to their bedroom.

He dropped her on the bed and turned to dim the lights and strip off his suit jacket.

"No," he ordered. "Let me."

He crawled on top of the bed. Taking hold of her dress, he tugged it off eagerly. When he was down to her matching black bra and panties, his eyes flared with hunger. He ran his hand over the embroidered surface of the bra and then started tugging. Hard. A loud ripping sound filled the air.

"Oh, sorry, that was cute," he murmured.

He dropped an apologetic kiss on the top of her head before pulling down her panties. He tossed them away before leaning over to stroke the tall black leather boots she was wearing.

"Keep these on," he said huskily, running his fingers along her leather-covered calves and up over her naked thighs.

Her breath caught, but Calen stopped before he reached the area that ached for his touch the most. Instead, his finger splayed on her thighs and curled until he was gripping her legs.

His eyes locked with hers. "Baby, can I tie you up?" he asked.

Maia froze. Briefly, apprehension tightened her chest, and she had to breathe in deeply before she realized she wasn't truly afraid. Just startled…and a little aroused.

Why not? She trusted Calen.

"Okay, let's try it," she whispered.

He shot her a sexy grin before hopping off the bed to dig through his closet. He came back with some of his neckties clutched in his hand. After wrapping one silky tie around her wrists, he checked the knot before tying it to the headboard. He tossed the other one away.

"I was going to blindfold you too, but I think I would rather see your eyes when you are at my mercy," he growled.

Maia's heart pounded as she tested her restraints. Her hands weren't that tightly bound, but she couldn't move them much. With her hands over her head, her breasts were lifted higher as if she was offering them to Calen.

And he soon took advantage. His large hands covered the small peaks, twisting and kneading gently until he pinched her nipples hard enough to make her cry out. It didn't really hurt, but the sensation was intense.

Her already warm body grew hotter. She could feel herself become wetter as Calen crawled over her like a predatory cat. Except for his shoes, he was still dressed. He lowered his body and her brain went into sensory overdrive as the rough texture of his shirt made contact with her naked breasts.

She didn't understand why it was so hot that he was clothed and she was naked, but her brain was threatening to melt down when he rocked forward and the fabric of his pants abraded the softness between her legs.

"We're going to ruin your suit," she said, in a tone suspiciously close to a squeal.

Calen laughed, the husky sound vibrating through her. "Don't worry about that. I have plenty of others," he said, working his way down her body. "You only worry about this."

He parted her legs with firm strong hands and lowered his head between them.

Maia's eyes closed in ecstasy as Calen's lips showered kisses all over her pussy, stopping to nibble on the lips before his tongue began to lick in long sure strokes. She could almost hear the blood pounding in her veins and would have sworn that her heartbeat had moved from her chest to her pussy, where her lover was using his mouth and hands to make her mindless.

Her legs shifted restlessly, and her hands trembled in the restraints. She could hear someone moaning in time with his rhythm and was startled to realize it was her.

The pressure built and built, until the pulsing pleasure tightened like a bowstring. After a few heartbeats, it broke and she cried out, "Oh God, Calen!" as she thrashed her head against the pillow.

Maia came back to herself reluctantly when Calen yanked down his zipper and pulled out his cock. He parted her legs roughly and crawled between them, guiding himself to her small silky entrance. He stared down at her face as started to work himself inside her.

"*Shit*," he groaned. "You are so tight. It's like taking a virgin every single time," he panted as he worked his full length inside of her.

Maia could only whimper as he slowly impaled her. Calen did have to be careful each time he entered her. He was too big for her petite frame, but she couldn't help but find the contrast between them exciting. He towered over her when they were standing. Even when he was above her on the bed, his size overwhelmed her, and she felt a thrill of sexual fear being at the mercy of such a large, muscular man.

But she knew in her heart that he would never hurt her.

"BEG ME TO STOP, LITTLE NYMPH," Calen panted as he continued to work himself in and out of her.

Maia's tight sheath gripped and fought him at the same time—as if she was simultaneously trying to push him out and keep him in. It fueled the fantasy he was creating with her boots and bound hands.

"What?" she gasped as her body was carried up and down with Calen's thrusts.

"I want you to beg me to stop fucking you...you tricksy little fey."

His voice was ragged with an edge of desperation and Maia's entire body tightened in response. Calen groaned when she gripped him even harder.

"Please, please stop, sir," Maia said.

"*Sir*? I like that. Beg sir for mercy. Tell him not to take your virginity," he hissed.

"But you've already—"

"Doesn't feel like it. Now beg."

She obliged him. She begged and pleaded, weaving a fantasy around him that had him pumping into her in fast hard strokes. He swore under his breath. Maia made him hot when he was stone cold sober. But like this, with her warm and aroused from the alcohol, and he was burning up. He hadn't even been able to undress properly.

Having her tied to his bed, at his mercy, was satisfying in a primal and unfamiliar way. The sharp edge of his need urged him on until he was pumping into her harder than he ever had before.

Luckily for him, Maia was with him all the way.

The more she pretended to beg for mercy, the more force he used to hold her down and take her. But she didn't object, instead she wrapped her legs around his pumping hips, digging her boot heels into his flexing buttocks.

Lost in his own personal paradise, he fought to last a little longer.

———

PLEASURE MOUNTED as Calen ground into her harder. Though it hurt a little, the pressure inside her built higher as she tried to clamp down and hold him inside of her. She didn't want to let him go.

Unable to hold it off, her inner muscles began to flutter and spasm. A heartbeat later, she cried out as her whole body convulsed around him. Calen's cock swelled and pulsed inside of her as he let out a hoarse shout. It felt like he was pumping an endless amount of his seed straight into her open, waiting womb.

He stayed suspended over her for a long minute before he finally rolled over and collapsed next to her.

Maia whimpered slightly as Calen lay next to her without moving to release her bindings. She twitched her arms and nudged him with her hip. "Sorry, baby," he panted. "I'll let you go, just give me a minute."

It actually took several minutes, but when he finally untied her he kissed her wrists, rubbing them gently before pulling her on top of him so that her back was to his front.

Maia was limp as Calen raised his knees and pulled her closer, shifting until her legs were over his, her buttocks against his softening erection. Lovingly, he put his arms around her, his hands cupping her breasts, tracing a line over them and down her waist. His hands rested there, and she was suddenly aware of what he was doing.

Calen was holding her in this position, with her legs up, to increase the chances for fertilization. He was trying to make sure she conceived his child.

The realization that Calen was, at this moment, trying to put a baby inside of her made Maia slightly dizzy. And conflicted. Deep down, she knew she wanted his baby. She wanted to give him ten babies. But she couldn't shake the louder more practical voice in her head lecturing her that she was too young, and there was still so much she wanted to accomplish in her life before she had children.

And she didn't know Calen as well as she should.

And that's what's actually bothering you. Not the fact he wants children, but that he wants them now.

She had always wanted a baby, after all. He hadn't been wrong about that. But she'd never had a boyfriend before, and financially there had been no possibility that she'd be able to care for a child on her own. But Calen was wealthy. A baby wouldn't be a burden to him. He was also very open and intensely affectionate.

And I'm going to be married to him in a few days. Soon I'll know almost everything about him. But if there were any surprises coming her way, she might be pregnant before she became aware of them. Then it would be too late.

"I'm sorry I can't let you out for a bachelorette party," Calen said, distracting her from her troubled thoughts. "Especially since it looks like I can't talk Liam out of throwing me a bachelor party. I know Maggie and Peyton were dead set on taking you out if we were doing something."

"Don't worry. I don't know them well enough yet for me to comfortable with them all on my own at something like that. I wouldn't want them throwing me a bachelorette party. Especially with Tahlia being away. Also, I get to blame you so they don't think I'm the bad guy or some freaky closet case," she said cheekily over her shoulder.

"You're welcome, I guess. But I am sorry. There would be too many variables, and I don't want to make things harder for your security team than it already is." He was quiet for a minute. "Hey...why didn't you mention that Chang was gay?"

"I don't know. I didn't think it was a big deal."

"If you had mentioned it, I would have had him over sooner. Not Wesley, but the gay guy is welcome," he said magnanimously, the possessive note in his voice sending a warm thrill down her spine.

"I had a crush on him before I realized he was gay," she said innocently.

Calen's hands clenched in her hair, and he tugged on it gently until her ear was next to his mouth.

"You like to play with fire don't you, baby?" he asked before he bit her ear. She squealed slightly and tried to wiggle away, but he held her firmly to him. "I can't believe you liked that skinny little drip of a kid."

Maia laughed. "He was nice to me and I was very shy. I am *still* shy. If we hadn't met the way we did, then I would never have had the courage to talk to you. If I'd seen you at your club, I would have been afraid to get caught even looking in your direction," she said honestly. "And I sort of knew Chang was gay before I officially found out. He was safe to like."

"Well, it's not safe now," Calen growled. "I may have to rescind his invitation."

She giggled and patted his hand. "Don't bother. How could anyone compete with you?" she teased, but deep down she meant it.

Mollified, Calen held her close and continued to stroke her stomach. Maia looked at him a touch nervously, but she didn't move off of him and eventually she drifted off to sleep in his arms.

CHAPTER 20

*T*he day of the wedding was hectic. Maia was woken by the arrival of the hairstylist and make-up artist Calen hired. He had spent the night at the Caislean, presumably sleeping off the hangover from his bachelor party the night before.

The day before, she had met his friends, Alex and Sergei, at the gourmet lunch Liam hosted at the hotel. Sergei kissed her on both cheeks and broke into a stream of Russian that made Calen walk over to him to pry his hands off her. Both Alex and Sergei laughed heartily.

"The shoe's on the other foot now," Alex drawled, and they all laughed at their private joke, refusing to elaborate for the others.

She strongly suspected their laughter had something to do with Alex's wife. Elynn wasn't what she was expecting. She was as small as Maia and extremely friendly. They instantly found many things in common and hit it off. Both Alex and Calen seemed pleased that they liked each other.

While the hairdresser tortured her with his brushes, Davis and the other bodyguards wandered the apartment, talking on their earpieces, and looking as though they were organizing security for a presidential visit instead of getting ready to drive her to the Caislean. She watched them with an air of amused detachment as her hair was tugged, twisted and tied up on her head.

Given how painful it was to achieve, she had expected the updo hairstyle to be a twist tight enough to give her a faux facelift. Instead, it was a lovely pile of loose curls befitting a fairy princess. Once her make-up was done, the hair stylist worked several delicate white orchids in her hair and helped her slip into the fairy wedding dress.

Maia stared into the mirror. It was hard to believe that the person staring back at her was herself. The dress made the most of her slight curves and her hair actually looked nice, instead of the wild untamable mop that was usually on her head. The make-up also made her look otherworldly. It emphasized her eyes, making them look huge. Altogether, the effect was a little startling, but she knew Calen would love it.

And she was right.

I'M MARRIED, Calen thought with satisfaction.

Furthermore, his little nymph of a bride might even be pregnant right now. He sat back, drinking a scotch with Liam and Sergei as he watched Maia dance with Trick.

The reception was in full swing. It was small for the size of the ballroom, but he didn't care. With the exception of Giancarlo, who hadn't been able to get out the sensitive merger talks he was in the middle of, everyone he cared about was here.

Almost.

His father had left early. The old man had made an appearance at the ceremony with Jimmy and his cousin Darren. Colman had given Maia a thoroughly disconcerting once over that had gotten Calen's temper up. He had put his arms around Maia to hold her closer to him, but when his father finally spoke to congratulate them, he had been cordial enough.

"Congratulations, young lady," Colman said, staring at Maia intently.

Maia had been tense under his hands, but she sounded completely normal when she replied. "Thank you. I'm so glad you were able to come, given the short notice."

Colman's responding smile was almost a smirk, but he didn't say anything else. Shortly after, he and Darren had left. After they were gone, Maia relaxed and was now having the best time, dancing, laughing, and drinking with his friends and their families.

As predicted, Maia and Elynn had gotten on like a house on fire. They had already exchanged emails and friended each other on Facebook. He'd watched the two of them talking earlier, comfortably aware that his infatuation for anyone who wasn't Maia was nonexistent now.

Calen had snapped a few pictures of himself with his bride, which he'd uploaded to her Facebook page. He'd made it public for the night, in case the Russians were monitoring it. Given his father's cameo appearance, that was probably unnecessary, but he wasn't taking any chances.

"You are very lucky, my friend," Sergei said in Russian as he sat down at the table next to him. "I think your bride suits you very well...even if your method of securing her was a bit unorthodox."

Sergei had been told the whole story as soon as Calen picked him up at the airport. The large Russian had been troubled until he'd realized how much Calen wanted to marry Maia. Like the others who were aware of 'the collection,' he'd gotten the picture once he'd finally met her.

"Yes, I think she's getting used to the idea of being my wife," he answered, his eyes following his bride as she danced.

She was a good dancer.

Sergei smirked. "I hope so, given that we are currently *at* your wedding."

Calen grinned and downed more scotch. "And what about you? Did your off-limits girl ever get within reach?"

Sergei frowned darkly and said nothing. Calen stared at him with a raised eyebrow until he cracked.

"*No.*"

"No? Come on, what is the situation there?" he asked

Sergei frowned again and swore softly in Russian. "She works for me. She's off limits."

"Since when has that stopped you?"

"I don't hook up with my employees," Sergei protested while nursing his vodka.

"All right, I know you don't, but you could make an exception. You've been interested in this girl for a while, and it hasn't gone away."

Sergei mumbled something and looked away.

"What was that?"

Sergei sighed—a long drawn out noise of suffering. He downed the rest of his vodka and refilled the glass. "I said I *already* made a pass at her, and she wasn't interested."

Calen scoffed. "Are you sure?"

"*Yes.*"

"Does she have a boyfriend?"

"No."

"A girlfriend?"

"*No.* She has no one to my knowledge."

"Weird. I've never known a straight and single woman to turn you down."

"Well, this one did," Sergei growled as he downed the next vodka in one gulp.

Calen clapped his friend sympathetically on the shoulder before he went to claim Maia for another dance. She had danced with Liam, Trick, and Chang, as well as with all the girls in one of those circles they seemed to spontaneously form whenever music was playing.

"All all-right love?" he asked her once he had her securely in his arms.

Maia flushed a delicious shade of pink and nodded. Her eyes wandered for a moment, and then she looked up at him questioningly. She leaned up on her tiptoes and whispered in his ear.

"Does Liam know Peyton is in love with him?"

Calen looked over at his friend. Liam was dancing with Peyton. The look on her face was unmistakable. It was a little painful to see.

He sighed. "No, and don't tell him."

"Wasn't planning on it. But it's kind of obvious."

"It's an open secret. The only one who doesn't seem to be aware of it is Liam himself," he said.

Maia's hand gripped his as they danced. "Why hasn't anyone told him? Don't you think they would make a good couple? Peyton's awesome," she said enthusiastically.

He smiled down at her indulgently. "You've become a fan in a short time."

His bride shrugged, "She's smart and kind and beautiful. And she's *not* into you. Of course I like her."

Calen laughed. "I'm aware of her many virtues, but her and Liam—it's not going to happen."

Maia frowned. "Why not?"

"Let's just say Peyton wouldn't be able to handle Liam. That's assuming he could ever see her as anything more than an unofficial little sister since she's Maggie's best friend. He would only end up hurting her. Trust me. It's better if she finds someone nice and normal like Maggie did."

Maia wrinkled her nose at him, but she decided to drop it. After a beat, she leaned in close as if she was going to tell him another secret. "I'm glad your father left early."

"So am I. Not that I don't love him as a son should...but it's complicated."

"Cause of the chilling and terrifying?" she whispered.

Calen's eyes widened as he looked down at her. Most people didn't see his father's true nature underneath the facade. He was a round-faced older man with thin hair who gave off the appearance of being everyone's favorite uncle. Calen didn't look like him at all. He most strongly resembled his mother's father—who was thankfully blessed with a full head of hair till his dying day at eighty-six years old.

"I know it's hard to believe now, but there is more to him than the bits that are terrifying," he assured her. "And when he gets on board and accepts that our marriage is real, he won't be so intimidating. In fact, I suspect he'll become your greatest supporter then."

"That is what you're betting on, right?" she asked as he whirled her around.

He was so much taller than her that she almost spun right out of his arms. It was easier for him to pick her up and dance with her suspended in his arms than for them to waltz the normal way, so he did just that, much to the amusement of their audience. Maia wrapped her arms around him and ignored the cheers and the hoots.

He kissed her hungrily. "Forget about my father and everyone else tonight. Everyone but me, that is," he ordered her as he swung her in a tight circle.

Judging from her smile, it was an order she was happy to follow.

CHAPTER 21

$\mathcal{M}$aia and Calen had returned from their Italian honeymoon more than a month ago, and she was settling into married life with surprising ease. Mostly.

It wasn't *all* completely natural. Occasionally she did have moments when she couldn't believe what her life had become. Living with someone was enough of a shock, but being married to a rich sex god was enough to give day-to-day life a surreal tinge.

That being said, Calen was actually pretty easy to live with. The only real complaints she had were minor.

She wished they had similar schedules. Calen had meetings in the afternoon and often went to check on his clubs at night. He had two in New York and the local one in Boston that he monitored personally. But he tried to keep time away from home to a minimum. The only exception had been a two-day trip to Miami to see his friend Sergei when the big Russian had gone on a drunken bender.

The rest of the time, Calen stayed close, checking on his other clubs by video chatting with his managers from his office. He still came home for dinner, but sometimes he had to go out afterwards whenever any issues arose at Siren. He came home late those nights.

But no matter what time he arrived, he still set an alarm to kiss her goodbye every morning, a small act that never failed to move her.

The only other problem was his insistence that she not go out at night, even with her bodyguards. According to his father, the Russians had backed off, but Calen wasn't taking any chances. If she was invited out, she couldn't go without him. She hadn't socialized much before meeting Calen, so Maia honestly didn't mind that much. But she could see it becoming an issue in the future.

However, at the moment, Tahlia was preoccupied with something and Chang was busy preparing for his thesis defense, so she wasn't actually missing any opportunities to go out with them anyway. But it would have been nice to be able to accept the invitations Maggie and Peyton frequently extended to her for a girl's night out when they had dinner with them at the Caislean.

Maggie's husband often joined them for dinner at the hotel. He was a good-looking man who doted on his young wife. He and Calen got along surprisingly well—although not well enough for Calen to confide in him the true circumstances of their marriage.

Liam had nixed the idea of taking Jason into their confidence. He didn't want his brother-in-law to have that kind of conflict of interest. Calen would never cooperate with the authorities if it endangered her, and Liam didn't want Jason to have to lie to his superiors.

At those dinners, Calen made it clear he wouldn't let Maia out of his sight long enough for a night out on the town. Maggie and Peyton made a point of teasing him about it whenever they saw him.

"Jesus, Calen. You have to let up with the caveman act," a flushed and tipsy Maggie had teased insistently at dinner last week. "You can let Maia off the leash for one night!"

Calen laughed. "We're newlyweds. Give us a little more time alone, and soon I'll treat you all to a night out at Siren. The complete VIP package. I promise."

"I swear he must keep Maia locked up in some sort of sexual dungeon when were not around," a mostly sober Peyton had whispered loudly in Maggie's ear.

Everyone had started laughing, and Maia blushed. Little did the girls know that their accusation had a ring of truth...

"Do you want a pudding before dinner?" Maia asked without turning around when she heard Calen step off the elevator that night.

She was digging around the refrigerator. In the short time they'd been married, she'd become a firm believer in dessert before dinner, a bad habit she was trying to get Calen to adopt. But he was too disciplined to go for it, although he did think it was cute when she indulged. He was always encouraging her bad habits—he insisted she didn't have enough of them.

"Calen? Pudding?" Maia repeated hopefully.

But he didn't respond to her offer of something sweet. He was hungry for something else.

"Well, what do we have here?" Calen murmured from behind her. "A hungry wood nymph stealing from me."

Maia straightened and slowly turned around. Her face was suffused with guilt. "I'm s-s-sorry, sir. I was just so hungry," she stammered, closing the refrigerator door behind her.

Calen had taken off his suit coat and was standing behind her, arms akimbo, a hard expression on his face. He walked up to her and slammed his hands on either side of her head. Startled, Maia jumped.

"You've made a big mistake stealing from me, little one," Calen murmured, his voice predatory. "But you are going to pay me back. I'm going to make sure of it."

Maia knew exactly what he wanted...so she gave it to him.

She ran.

Darting under his arm, she rounded the kitchen counter, through the dining room and into the living room. Calen pounded after her, and she ran around the couch, putting it between them. He stalked her then, shifting around the furniture slowly as she moved to stay behind the protective barrier.

"Please don't hurt me, sir. I'm sorry I stole from you. I won't ever do it again," she pleaded. "Please let me go."

She must have been convincing, because guilt flared in Calen's eyes. But it only lasted a second before lust clouded them once more. He feinted right, and she fell for it. He was on her in seconds.

Calen grabbed and swung her around, forcing her lips to his. When she struggled and twisted her head away from the kiss, he dropped her down on the couch a little roughly and climbed on top of her.

"I'm not going to hurt you. Not if you cooperate like a good little nymph. Because you're mine now. Mine to keep, mine to fuck...mine to breed," he whispered in her ear as he lifted her skirt and yanked her panties down until they fell from her body.

Maia sucked in a deep breath. That last part wasn't playacting anymore. Calen meant every word. He was so possessive, and she loved it. That he wanted her that much was overwhelming, it made her want to promise him anything. But she was still too hesitant to make those promises aloud.

Not that Calen was waiting for an answer. He took hold of her flailing arms with one hand and used the other to roughly part her legs. "You *are* mine now. Do you understand?" he growled as he positioned himself between her legs.

Maia nodded automatically. That wasn't in the script. She wasn't supposed to agree so easily. But the truth was impossible to deny.

Too caught up in their game to notice she was breaking character, Calen unzipped and took hold of his already swollen cock. With a slow deliberate move, he ran it up and down over her silky entrance, and she whimpered aloud. She was so wet her fluids were running down her body to the couch cushions. Beyond the capacity to be embarrassed, she twisted in his embrace, forcing him to hold her still.

He probed her small entrance with the bulbous head of his cock and Maia hissed and bucked in response. "Please don't. I've never had a man there," she whispered as she locked eyes with him.

Calen stared down into her flushed face, his eyes heating. He *loved* it when she played along.

"I can't tell you how pleased I am to hear that. But I will be filling that tight little hole because it belongs to me now," he whispered as he fisted a hand in her hair. "Your untouched little cunt is mine—all mine

—and I'm the only man you will ever have," he promised hoarsely as he held her down and pushed into her slowly.

Maia writhed and tried to push him away, crying out as she pleaded with him to stop.

CALEN PUSHED and worked his cock into Maia slowly, as he always had to with her. She was so small and tight it did feel like he was taking her innocence every single time. And it would always feel like that given how small she was compared to him. He had to enter her carefully, but it was worth it for this feeling.

She gripped him so firmly it made him want to explode the second he felt her tight clinging walls around his cock. But he didn't stop until his balls were flush with Maia's ass. He was so deep he was touching her womb. Hoping he wasn't hurting her, he withdrew and pistoned back inside her a little harder.

"You're so fucking tight," he panted. "I swear you're gonna kill me."

Maia only moaned in response. He worked in and out of her sheath until she stretched a little more and he was able to move in and out more easily. Meanwhile, Maia whimpered and continued to plead for him to stop.

Her cries and protests fueled his hunger, and he took her more roughly, slamming in and out of her slick passage with some gasps and moans of his own. He moved the hand twisted in her hair, using it to force her head up so he could plunge his tongue into her mouth.

"Say it. Say you belong to me," he said between kisses as he held her hands down tighter against the couch cushions while grinding his cock into her soft wet core.

"I'm yours. I'm yours...Master," Maia whispered in his ear.

Calen's rhythm stuttered. He hadn't asked her to call him Master, but it was the right thing for her to say. Her instinct always served her well when they were together. He didn't need to hear anything else. His cock swelled and pulsed in response, and he came with a shout.

His release triggered her own. Maia contracted and pulsed around him and she gasped raggedly.

He collapsed on top of her, breathing in her soft floral scent as he struggled to recover enough to move.

"Well, fuck. I guess we don't have to ask if the marriage has actually been consummated anymore," Darren McLachlan said from somewhere behind them.

Underneath him, Maia froze. Calen whipped his head around to look over the back of the couch. His cousin Darren was standing in the foyer smirking. Jimmy was next to him, looking at everywhere but Calen with a studiously blank expression.

"What the fuck!" he roared as he withdrew, pulling Maia's skirt down as he went. They couldn't see much of her from where they were. Which was good, or he would have to kill them both. "What the hell are you two doing here?" he growled, scrambling up and turning his back to pull his pants up.

Once he was safely zipped, he grabbed the throw Maia kept on the couch and tossed it over her. He put a restraining hand on her shoulder to signal that he didn't want her to get up before stalking around the couch to confront their unwanted guests.

"Sorry," Jimmy said, coughing apologetically and looking away. "Your man Davis let us up."

Un-fucking-believable.

"Call first next time. Or better yet, just call and don't ever fucking show up here again," he spat out as Darren stood on his tiptoes to try and see over the couch, still smirking.

Calen felt a murderous rage rise up inside him. He stepped forward to knock that fucking grin off Darren's face. Unfazed, his cousin rocked on his heels, and Calen stopped in front of the couch, blocking Maia from sight.

"Colman would like you to come over for dinner tonight. He sent us to deliver the invitation personally," Darren said.

"Why wouldn't he pick up the fucking phone instead?" Calen seethed, staring at the two men with his hands on his hips.

Jimmy stepped in. "Darren, give me a minute. Calen why don't we talk in the office for a second?"

Calen scowled. "I'm not leaving him alone with my wife."

Darren dropped the smirk and frowned instead. "I'm not going to hurt her," he said, sounding outraged.

"I don't care. You stay in sight," he said. He stroked Maia's hair as she peeked over the back of the sofa before bashfully ducking back down. "Be right back, baby," he said before leading the men to the office.

He threw the doors open. Jimmy followed him in while Darren sighed exaggeratedly and leaned against the bar across from the doors. Calen didn't like that Darren could still see Maia if she sat up, but at least the fucker wasn't moving closer to her.

Standing near Calen's desk, Jimmy waited till he was close enough to him before leaning in conspiratorially. "Look, the old man did send us to bring you to dinner. But he also told us to take a look around. You know, for signs," he said.

"What signs?" he asked, scowling.

"Signs you are *actually* married," Jimmy said with a shrug. "You know how he is. Colman thinks you're a little soft sometimes. He thought you were playing the hero to save this girl, keeping her close to throw off the Russians. But he's been watching, and you surprised him."

"Surprised him how?" Calen asked, rolling his eyes, resigned to the fact his father was keeping tabs on him.

"You haven't been acting like a single man since you got hitched. You're acting like a newlywed. You hired bodyguards for the little wife, and you buy her presents almost every day. You took her to Italy for a honeymoon where you met up with that wop friend of yours in Rome."

"*Don't call Gio names,*" Calen hissed between gritted teeth.

"Sure, whatever," Jimmy said placatingly. "My point is you took Maia all the way to Rome to see him. And then you took her to Venice to spend even more money on her. You introduced her to all your friends and take her out to see them a lot. And you ignore other women when they come up to you at the club. Then there's the fact you rush home every night. Actually, you don't spend any real time in any of your clubs anymore. You might want to change the last though. Your da doesn't want you to neglect your business."

Calen rolled his eyes. "Tell my da how I run my clubs is not his concern. There's no fucking reason for him to watch me anymore. I'm really married, and everything is *fine*."

Except he wasn't fine. He'd known his father was probably spying on him and Maia, but he hadn't been aware of how closely they'd been monitored.

Jimmy held up a hand. "No need to go off. Colman is only keeping an eye in case the Russians make a play. But you know how he is about wanting grandkids. He only gave the girl a quick look at the wedding 'cause he thought you were faking it. But if she's going to be the mother of his grandbabies, he wants to get to know her better. So bring her to dinner. What's the harm?"

Calen didn't want to agree, but if it made his father bring Maia into the fold that much sooner, he had no choice. "All right," he muttered, turning and walking out of the office.

"Shall we go?" Darren asked, straightening with a game show hostess gesture to the door. He leaned in close as the others approached. "And don't bother to clean up. Your dad'll wanna see her like that," he whispered.

Enraged, Calen stepped toward him threateningly, determined to pound his cousin into the ground. He didn't care that Darren was a father of two now. Those kids would be better off without their asshole of a father.

He was about to go for the throat when Jimmy rushed between them. "Why don't you and the little woman go get changed for dinner. We'll wait for you downstairs," the older man said hurriedly as he shoved Darren to the elevator.

Before Calen could tell them they weren't going to dinner anymore, the elevator doors closed behind them.

"Are they gone?" Maia asked.

He turned around, and the anger slipped away when he saw her peeking over from behind the top of the couch. She looked embarrassed, but reasonably composed. If she had looked hurt or humiliated, he would be on his way down to the basement to tear Darren a new one. But she seemed fine. His fairy was resilient.

"Yeah," he said. "Don't worry. We don't have to go dinner tonight. We can do it some other time. I'll call my father right now."

"Won't he be mad?" she asked, worrying her lower lip with her teeth.

"I don't care. If he had called instead of sending my asshole of a cousin, I'd say let's go, but I'm pissed now so they can wait downstairs all night for all I care."

Maia thought about it. "Maybe we should go," she said unexpectedly.

"Why?"

"If we don't, I'll just end up worrying about it. It might be better to get it over with. You said we'd have to eventually anyway."

And he had. But Calen had expected that Maia would have to be noticeably pregnant before his father invited her into his home. Either he'd come around early because of everything Jimmy said, or something else had come up...something about the Russians. If that was the case, they needed to know.

"All right, let's hop in the shower," he finally agreed.

"Do we have time for a shower?" she asked as he ushered her to their room.

"Those assholes can wait."

CHAPTER 22

arren was annoyed, but not surprised, when Calen kept him and Jimmy waiting for the better part of an hour before meeting them in the garage.

When he did come down, he allowed him and Jimmy to drive them to his father's house with surprisingly little argument. However, the prick insisted that his bodyguards meet them in a few hours to bring them back. Calen wanted to be able to leave at the moment of his choosing.

"The less I see of you the better," he'd growled at Darren.

Darren sat up front with Jimmy as they drove. In the backseat, Calen sat with his new bride, completely ignoring him despite his continued attempts to get another rise of out of him.

When his formerly ultra-cool and reserved cousin nuzzled little Maia's ear, the girl blushed and ducked her head. Then she looked up at Calen and said something that made him laugh softly.

"You know, I thought he was crazy when he said he was going to marry her," Jimmy murmured quietly, "but it kind of makes sense now doesn't it?"

Jimmy had also noticed Calen's absorption with his new bride.

Darren wasn't a fan of his cousin, but he had to concede the girl was hot. If you liked them small—which he didn't.

"Yeah, I guess. If you like fucking a Christmas elf," he muttered, underplaying the sexual energy the couple in the back seat was generating.

"I don't see him complaining," Jimmy remarked.

Darren peeked at the couple at the back seat. Now Calen was playing with the girl's hair.

"No," he finally agreed.

He spent the rest of the trip checking them out. Calen didn't bother to look over at him once, not even to give him the stink eye.

However the couple had started out, they were now totally wrapped up in each other.

DINNER WAS A CASUAL AFFAIR. Colman McLachlan had a lovely spacious home in South Boston. The neighborhood was nothing like Maia imagined. Calen had told her that Southie was starting to move past its blue-collar roots, and it appeared he was right.

At the house, Maia was introduced to other cousins and Darren's wife, Mary Margaret. She was showing off a new baby, a cute little girl only a few weeks old that everyone fussed over. Mary Margaret herself was getting around in crutches because she'd broken her leg a few months ago.

As for Calen's dad, Colman, he greeted her politely and then walked off to converse privately with Darren and his son for a while. After a few minutes, Calen came back to her to give her a tour of the first floor of the house. Then Colman called everyone together for dinner.

An assortment of other men and their families joined them for the actual meal. She didn't have to ask Calen who they were. Some were obviously relatives, but others had a look that screamed gangster. Colman's 'employees' mixed with the others, like one big extended family.

People were everywhere, in the kitchen at a small table, at the bar, and in the living room. They were even sitting on the stairs leading to the second story. And no one was shy about checking her out. Every last one gave her an obvious inspection, but Calen's hovering ensured everyone stayed polite.

After the meal, most of the employees melted away. The rest of the family drifted into the living room and den. The men sat around and drank scotch while Maia played with the new baby for a while before Mary Margaret had her put to bed. Afterwards, the two women made polite small talk. Mary Margaret asked Maia about the wedding and their honeymoon in Italy.

Maia and Calen had visited his friend Giancarlo in Rome and then had spent a romantic few days in Venice. Calen had spoiled her rotten there. Venice was a shopping mecca, with countless high-end stores and boutiques. Her wardrobe had expanded exponentially, as had her collection of jewelry, despite her protests.

She didn't mention that last to Mary Margaret in case the other woman told Darren. She didn't want to feed the competitiveness between the two cousins. Or between herself and Mary Margaret, for that matter. The older woman was polite enough, but from their conversation, Maia sensed she was a little shallow.

Throughout the evening, Maia was aware of Colman's dark eyes following her. She tried to forget that she was being evaluated and judged, but it was difficult. Eventually, she wandered away and sought refuge in one of the other rooms on the first floor. She was surprised to find a little boy playing by himself in a mostly empty room. He was between two or three years old, and he looked a lot like Calen and Darren.

"Hi there," Maia said, crouching on the ground next to the little boy.

When the boy didn't look up, she waved in his line of vision. He looked up at her, and she was rewarded with a huge smile. He looked a lot like Calen then. Immediately hooked, she smiled back at him and sat down.

Maia lost track of time playing with the lively toddler. He alternated between crawling all over her and assembling his blocks with loud exclamations. When they fell over, he industrially stacked them back up. She made a game of it, and the time passed quickly. They were so engrossed they didn't notice when they acquired an audience. Eventually a noise alerted her to their presence, and she swung her gaze up to look at Calen, his father, and cousin right before the toddler tackled her.

"Mmmph," Maia grunted as she toppled over.

The baby was small, but very dense and heavy. Calen moved forward to pull him off and help Maia off the floor. Nervous, she smoothed her dress down and walked over to the other men.

"I see you met Darren Jr.," Colman said.

There was a strange tension in the air. Telling herself she was being paranoid, Maia turned to the brooding Darren. "Oh, is he yours, too? How old is he?" she asked politely.

For some reason, he looked annoyed. "He's two and half," Darren muttered eventually.

"He's a beautiful boy. And so smart for his age. You must be so...proud."

Maia's voice trailed off when Darren's expression turned thunderous. She quailed and fought the temptation to hide behind Calen.

"You don't have to say that," Darren said sharply.

Maia swallowed tightly but felt the need to clarify. "I only meant that he's very advanced for his age."

"Look here," Darren began, raising a finger in her face as he took a threatening step before her.

Maia would have dived behind Calen then if he hadn't forestalled her by placing a hand on her shoulder and drawing her back to his front.

"What do you mean, sweetheart?" he said, cutting Darren off.

He sounded a little confused.

Maia swallowed heavily. She reminded herself that Darren wasn't a threat as long as Calen was there. "Well, two and half is pretty young for numbers, but he can add and subtract. I don't think they're supposed to do that till they're three or four. I showed him a game I used to play with my neighbor and he was catching on quickly. My neighbor's son didn't do as well when he was a year older."

The men looked at each other, glances she couldn't read properly.

"Is something wrong?" she asked uncertainly.

"You don't have to lie. My son is...slow," Darren bit out.

Now it was her turn to be confused. "I don't understand. He's a little behind on his communication skills, but once you get him a tutor, things should get easier. He's not too young to start. I'm guessing you don't sign yourself?"

"What do you mean? What sign?" Calen asked while Colman's eyes dug into her.

Did they not know? Maia gestured around her ear. "A sign language tutor. Because he's...he's deaf."

Her announcement was met with complete silence.

"No, he's not," Darren said in disbelief.

Maia was genuinely confused now. "I...I think he is," she said, trying to sound certain, but it was hard when Darren was towering over her threateningly.

"Come here, baby," Calen said, putting little Darren down. "Come play your game with him."

Maia moved away from Darren senior as quickly as she could without seeming impolite. She sat in front of the blocks again and offered the toddler the first two blocks and then she showed him four fingers. When the baby added two more blocks to the pile, Maia clapped and smiled while Calen frowned and looked over at his father.

He crouched down and snapped his fingers behind the baby's head, but little Darren didn't turn around. Calen snapped again at the side of his head repeatedly. Again there was no response. Not as long as Calen snapped out of his line of vision. When Calen snapped in front of him little Darren finally noticed and grinned up at him.

"Well, I'll be god-damned. We're all a bunch of fucking idiots," Calen pronounced as Darren senior picked up his son and looked at him closely.

"Did you really not know?" Maia whispered to Calen as he took her hand and helped her up.

Calen gave his father a look as Darren stalked off with his son without a word.

"I think we should go now," he told him.

"Not yet," Colman replied while studying Maia. She was starting to feel like a bug under a microscope. "There is something I would like to show Maia," he said, offering her his hand.

Maia glanced at Calen, but he just shrugged. Fidgeting slightly, she took Colman's hand and he led her away. She followed him up the stairs and down a short hallway. When he arrived at the door on the end, he opened it and motioned for her to step inside.

"This was Calen's room when he was a boy," he said as he stepped inside behind her. "He had another when he was older, a bigger one farther from the master bedroom. I kept this one the way it was though."

Maia smiled softly as she took in the little racecar bed and the shelves full of toys. There were also drawings on the wall, very good ones. Calen was a skilled artist. He had never mentioned it at all. But that didn't surprise her. Her husband was surprisingly modest about some things.

She stepped closer to the picture he had drawn of a fairy in the garden. More masculine drawings of animals and transformers surrounded it, but the fairy was still there after all these years. She looked up to find Colman watching her quietly. His stare was unnerving, despite his friendly avuncular appearance.

"Calen says your mother was half-Irish. Do you know where her people are from?" he asked.

"Um, not really. Her mother lived in Kilkee in Clare County before she moved here. But I'm not sure if that's where her family was from."

Colman nodded. "We'll have to look into that." He walked over to an overloaded closet and dug around until he pulled out a thin book. "Do you and Calen plan on having children?" he asked bluntly.

Maia nodded a little too emphatically. "Yes, he wants them right away."

"*Seriously?*" Colman's face was a study in surprise.

"Yes."

"So you're trying for kids now?" he asked.

Maia flushed red, but she nodded again. This time, Colman gave her a genuine smile and handed her the thin volume. It was a Christmas-themed children's book. Next to Santa was a female elf with orange-gold hair and blue eyes.

Maia looked down at the book with her mouth slightly open. She caught Colman looking at her and snapped it shut as she sat down on the bed to flip through the book. The colorful pages showed how Angelina the Elf saved Christmas.

"He probably doesn't remember, because he wasn't much older than little Darren junior, but his mother used to read him that book almost every night. It was his favorite. After she died, I put it away. She used to tell him other stories too. Fairy stories. I thought he had forgotten all about that. But I guess there are some things you don't forget."

Maia's mouth twisted wryly, and she nodded. "I guess not."

CHAPTER 23

*M*aia decided not to give Calen the book right away. Christmas was a few months away, and though she had several things in mind for gifts, she wanted to give him the book on that day. If all went well, she would be pregnant by then, and that would add another gift to the pile.

Of course, she could be pregnant well before then at the rate she and Calen were going.

Unless he came home from one of his clubs too late, he made love to her at least twice a night during the week and more often on the weekends. His high sex drive had taken some getting used to, but as time went on she had grown more confident in her own sexuality. She kept up with him with gusto now.

She had even started to daydream about having a little baby, too. She blamed Darren's adorable little ones for taking her vague fantasies of future children and turning them into a full-blown case of baby lust.

Since she had alerted them to it, little Darren's deafness had been confirmed, and now a nice young man came by every weekday to teach the toddler and his mother sign language. They were also exploring the possibility of a cochlear implant.

Calen had explained that his son's inability to respond to him had caused Darren to neglect his son. A teenage cousin acted as nanny for him, which might have explained why no one had realized why the baby didn't respond when spoken to. Darren senior hadn't liked for people to think his son was mentally deficient, so he'd actively discouraged other family members from spending time with him.

Maia had thought that was shameful, and Calen had agreed, but Darren hadn't listened when he had tried to discuss it with him before she came along. Their already tense relationship contributed to that. Darren treated everything Calen said with suspicion.

"Why? How did all of that start?" she asked him one night after they had made love.

In the darkness of their bedroom, Maia felt him shrug. "It's been that way for years. Since I decided not to go into business with the family."

"But wouldn't that have made Darren more comfortable and easier to get along with?"

Calen scoffed. "You'd think so, but he's insecure. I think he could have dealt with being third in line after me, but this way is somehow worse for him. Everyone knows that if I ever changed my mind, Da would give me Darren's place in a heartbeat. He resents that, but my reassurances that I want no part of the business only seem to make things worse."

Maia mulled that over. "Maybe it's because he interprets your refusal as a slight to what he and your family do."

Calen laughed. "The irony is that a lot of what they do is legal these days. Just not all of it."

After that, Maia hoped the situation between the cousins would improve. Little Darren's diagnosis seemed to make Darren more mellow. He could deal with a deaf son a lot better than one that was mentally disabled in some way. But Maia could still feel the tension between Darren and Calen when they saw each other. She and Calen went to Colman's place for dinner every other week. And, inevitably, at least once during the night, he and Darren got into it. They never came to blows, but it was a near thing sometimes. There didn't seem to be an easy fix for what was wrong between them.

Halloween came and went with a flurry of activity. Calen took her to two different parties, one at his club Sylph in New York and one that Liam and Trick threw at the Caislean New York. Both Maggie and Peyton were in attendance and the three of them had a lot of fun drinking and dancing. At least until she noticed Peyton's stricken expression when they walked by Liam dancing with some skinny blonde.

Liam's date was some other hotelier's daughter, and he seemed very interested in her. Aching with sympathy, Maia did her best to distract her new friend. The fact that she herself had been getting unpleasant looks from another woman herself at the party only increased her determination to leave. Maia convinced Calen to take the three of them back to his club. Once they were back at Sylph they promptly lost Liam and his date. Peyton didn't mention it later, but she gave her a tight hug at the end of the night.

Maia never found out who the unpleasant woman at the hotel party was. She assumed it was someone Calen used to date, but he didn't speak to the woman and she didn't want to ask.

THE WEEKS SLIPPED BY QUICKLY as Mrs. Calen McLachlan. She had a full and busy life with a wider circle of friends than she'd ever had. Though she didn't see Tahlia that much, she and Chang spent a lot of time with Maggie and Peyton. With her bodyguards discretely in tow, she attended various outings with them—brunch and shopping expeditions.

And eventually, after being repeatedly baited and teased by Maggie and Peyton, Calen finally made good on his promise of a girls-only night at Siren. Unfortunately, it was a disaster from the start.

The first sign it was going badly happened when Calen refused to stay home.

"I'm not going to get in your way, nymph, I promise. I'm going to be all the way upstairs in the manager's office the whole night," Calen said.

They had been arguing about it for ten minutes. Sighing, Maia relented. There was no way she was going to win. Calen did own the club.

"Will you at least ask Davis and Stephens to back off a little? They're so intimidating, and their presence distracts Maggie and Peyton. It's hard to relax around them."

"Nymph, half of their job is intimidation. They need to be visible in public so people know you're protected," he said, putting his hands on either side of her head.

He kissed her softly, but Maia made an effort not to weaken the way she usually did when he touched her.

"Please, Calen. I just want to have fun. And they're bringing some of their other girlfriends with them. It's hard to explain the presence of two huge bodyguards," she said, tugging at his hands.

Calen relented. "Okay. They back off tonight. But they're still going. I'll assign Stephens to the security office for the night. He'll monitor your group over the camera feeds. Davis will still be guarding you, but discreetly. It's the best I can do."

Maia knew that was the best deal she was going to get. "I'll take it," she said cheerfully, certain the evening was going to be a blast.

But the outing started on a sour note when the car Calen ordered arrived with Maggie, Peyton, and their two friends. Jane seemed nice, but Shelly was a bitch from word one.

"So your Calen's wife," Shelly said nasally, looking her up and down disparagingly.

"Hi," Maia said, settling into the car uncomfortably.

She hadn't expected the other girl to be so sour. Gratefully, she accepted a glass of champagne from Peyton and tried to not to let her dismay at Shelley's reception show on her face. She tried to talk to both Shelly and Jane, but only Jane responded politely to her questions. Shelly, on the other hand, spent the ride whispering in Jane's ear while looking at Maia from behind her own glass of champagne.

She's sneering at me.

Suddenly Maia felt small and ugly as she watched the tall and exotic Shelly adjust her electric blue handkerchief top. Lips pressed into a tight line, she tugged on the hem of her comparatively modest green silk dress.

"I'm so sorry about her," Peyton whispered in her ear as the car arrived at the club. "Shelly's just jealous. She's been trying to catch Calen's eye for years and failed miserably. But we thought she was over him. She's been saying she is for over a year now. I had no idea she would act like this. Maggie and I will make sure she behaves herself, or we'll leave her at home next time."

Maia thanked her a little weakly, but after that, she was oversensitive and self-conscious. Inside the club, it got worse. She started noticing how the other woman at the club looked at her—particularly the staff and women she assumed were regulars.

Everyone was curious about Calen's bride and judging from the dismissive looks she got, most of the women found her lacking. They were obviously asking themselves what someone like him saw in her. After trying and failing to have a good time at the roped off VIP booth Calen had reserved for them, Maia escaped to the bathroom to regroup. She hid in the stall for a while until she realized how cowardly she was being.

When she left the stall, there was only one other woman in the bathroom, a stranger in a short, fire-engine-red dress and matching spiked heels.

"Hello," Maia said, confused when the woman blocked her path to the sink. "Can I help you?"

The woman drew back her head and sneered. "I can't believe he married *you*. Look at you. You're nothing!"

The blood drained from Maia's face. Was this one of Calen's ex-girlfriends? She was about to ask, but before she could utter a word, Davis swept in. He moved between a stunned Maia and the woman and swept the stranger away with a hand on her arm.

"Hey! Let go," the woman said, struggling in Davis' grip.

But the bodyguard marched her out with a firm hand. He came

back in a minute later. "Are you all right?" he asked, concern all over his strong blunt features.

Maia looked down and shrugged. "I doubt that's the last time something like that will happen. I think I'm better off skipping girl's night altogether from now on."

First there had been that rude woman at the Halloween party and now this. How many more of Calen's castoffs was she going to have to deal with?

Davis frowned. He started to say something, but Maia waved him into silence and walked back out to the table. She sat down and grabbed her still-full drink, downing it in a single pull.

"That's the party spirit!" Maggie laughed, reaching over to clink glasses with her.

When Calen emerged from the manager's office a little later, Maia had more than enough alcohol inside her, and she was spoiling for a fight. She hadn't told the other ladies about the bathroom incident, but she was sure Davis had told Calen. And she was right—Calen came by their table with a peace offering.

"Compliments of the management," he said magnanimously as a waitress set up two ice buckets filled with champagne at their table.

The girls hooted and hollered in celebration and thanks, but Maia didn't say anything as Calen studied her carefully.

He leaned over. "You okay baby?" he asked. He sounded worried. She nodded and he smiled, reassured. "Enjoy the champagne ladies. I'll be back in an hour to collect my wife, so make the most of it,"

"Oh, come on, Calen," Maggie said. "It's still early!"

"I've lent her to you long enough. One more hour, then she's all mine again," he said, stopping for a kiss before walking away with a wave.

Maia felt cold inside as her husband kissed her in front of everyone. It felt like he was putting on a show for their audience. She bypassed the champagne and ordered a second cosmopolitan, which was quickly followed by a third.

CHAPTER 24

*F*rom across the crowded club floor, Timur watched McLachlan stop by the table full of pretty girls to offer the group champagne and say hello to his wife.

His wife.

The fucking Mic had married her. Maia Dahl was now Maia McLachlan. And according to Peter and his father, she was now out of his reach.

He had been arguing steadily with the pair about the bitch. His father had finally listened to his concerns, but it was too late. Colman McLachlan had refused their offer to reacquire the girl. But that didn't mean he was giving up.

Viktor was watching him watch the bitch. The beast wasn't happy. He didn't say anything—he usually didn't. But Timur could feel Viktor's judgment weighing on him, daring him to get up and go after the girl right now, so he'd have an excuse to drag him back home like some petulant child. His babysitter hadn't wanted to bring him to the club tonight. Viktor had actually opened his fucking mouth to complain in that voice that sounded like he was chewing gravel and nails. But Timur was still the Komarov's only son. And he was only watching. For now...

Timur had wanted to see the newlyweds together with his own eyes. His men had notified him as soon as the two had left McLachlan's castle in the sky. When they didn't go to the Caislean to their regular dinner and had come to the club instead, he'd made Viktor bring him here. The effort had been worth it. From what he could see, getting his hands on the girl might not be as hard as he thought.

There was trouble in paradise. The girl had been downing drinks for an hour, staring blankly, and avoiding the eyes of the other women. Even he could see her tension from way across the room.

The fancy clothes and expensive champagne weren't enough to make her happy. She was just another ungrateful bitch.

Then McLachlan emerged from his office upstairs. He joked with the girls at the table and then took Maia away, bodyguards in tow. The possessive way he touched her told Timur everything he needed to know about their relationship.

The girl's unhappiness was the key. If she disappeared at the right time, then everyone would think she'd run away, that she'd gotten tired of being McLachlan's pampered prisoner. Then he could take care of her the way he should have as soon as they'd caught her in the woods.

All he needed to do was pick his moment.

CHAPTER 25

he hour was over before she knew it. As promised, Calen came back to the table to say goodbye to the others before he quickly ushered her towards the car. Maia allowed herself one small satisfied sniff when he didn't even bother to look at Shelly as they left, despite the other woman's effusive parting.

As they approached the penthouse, Maia's sense of outrage finally lost steam. She started to question her right to be angry. It wasn't as if she could confront Calen about his past. It wouldn't be fair to do that to a normal boyfriend or husband. And given how they had come together, she might not even have a right to question his future.

If Calen grew bored and indulged in an indiscretion with some slutty club girl, what could she do? Sitting back and turning a blind eye to it didn't sit well with her...but it wasn't like she could leave him. She'd be trapped in a bad marriage for the rest of her life.

It was also bothering her that she couldn't hide anything from Calen. Under normal circumstances, he would never know that one of his exes had tried to confront her. Even Peyton, as unfortunate as her situation was, was able to hide how she felt when she saw Liam with someone else.

But with her minders Davis and Stephens shadowing her every

move, Maia could never hope to keep any of those humiliating moments from her husband.

CALEN WATCHED Maia anxiously as Davis drove them home from Siren. It was two a.m. and he was tired. He had spent most of the night in his office teleconferencing with his other managers in Vegas and Miami. Both of those clubs were experiencing problems with different suppliers, and a new competitor had opened across the street from the Vegas location. He wasn't worried about the club's viability, but he had still taken steps to promote the club's profile, including organizing a series of celebrity DJ's to come in a few times a month for the foreseeable future. But none of those annoyances was bothering him as much as Maia's silence.

He'd been worried when Davis had told him one of his former hookups, one that didn't even look familiar when Stephens pointed her out, tried to harass Maia by cornering her in the bathroom. It wasn't the first time something like that had happened, but Davis had been able to intercede before Maia was confronted on the other occasion at the Caislean Halloween party.

Shit. Things had been going so well lately between the two of them. Their relationship was everything he'd hoped it would be. Hell, it was better.

He'd gone down to check on Maia after Davis had told him what happened, but she had already sat in the middle of Maggie's group of girlfriends, and he hadn't wanted to pull her out of there to talk. Instead, he had personally delivered two complimentary bottles of Cristal to the group. The other women greeted the champagne with cheers, but Maia hadn't touched it. And now she wasn't talking to him beyond one-word answers to his questions.

He waited until they were back home before he broached the subject. Maia was heading to the bedroom when he grabbed her arm and turned her to face him.

"Baby, you're going to have to start talking to me sometime. Are you mad at me? Did I do something to upset you? Just tell me what it is," he said.

Maia's brows lifted at that, but she didn't reply.

"What? What aren't you telling me?" Calen asked. "Did something else happen?"

"No. All I want is to take a shower and go to bed."

He ran a hand roughly through his hair. "Look, I'm sorry that woman bothered you. You know that I would give anything to keep things like that from happening."

Maia sighed and looked down. "That's fine to say, but what can you actually do about it? You have a past. A rather extensive one when it comes to other women. How am I supposed to handle it? Other than not going to your clubs, which I don't intend on doing again."

Calen frowned, but since Maia wasn't looking at him, she missed it. "I don't want you to avoid my clubs for the rest of your life. I know it was pretty shitty for you tonight. All I can say is that these uncomfortable situations will pass the longer we are together. Soon people won't remember me without you."

Maia seemed to wilt before his eyes. "You didn't see how everyone was looking at me. And really, how can I expect anyone to take us seriously when we don't have a normal relationship? When we don't even have a real marriage?"

Calen froze, his heart sinking in his chest. "What did you say?"

Maia stayed quiet, eyes downcast.

"*What did you say?*" he yelled.

Maia started in surprise, eyes huge. He didn't blame her for being scared. His sudden fury had shocked even him. And he had never raised his voice to her.

She wouldn't look at him. "I said we don't have a real marriage," she whispered, her eyes on the floor.

Calen felt like the wind had been knocked out of him. "Is that how you really feel?"

Maia's voice was small but steady, "How else am I supposed to feel? I know I'm lucky that by some quirk you find me attractive, but you wouldn't have ever married me under normal circumstances. And when one of these women tries to call me out for being with you, what can I say or do to defend myself when we should never have happened in the first place?"

Calen took a deep breath and tried to calm down. Maia was explaining her concerns to him, and he owed it to her to listen with the same level of seriousness.

He honestly hadn't known how insecure she was about their relationship. Not even showing her his collection had convinced her that he couldn't have been happier to have her in his life. He should have realized it wasn't going to be that simple.

"I don't *ever* want to hear this kind of bullshit from you ever again. You are my wife, the only woman I want."

"For how long?" Maia said, sitting down heavily on the couch.

She looked so dejected.

"Forever," he said.

Maia looked at him uncertainly. "I want to believe you. It's just..." She shook her head.

"Shit," he muttered quietly, making Maia frown at him. He sighed. "I wasn't going to do this," he said rubbing his eyes with the back of his hand. "Come with me," he said, extending his hand.

When she didn't move he grabbed her hand and marched her to his office. He led her to his desk.

"Calen, I've seen your collection," she told him.

He ignored her and opened his laptop. He closed some windows and sat down at his desk chair, pulling her into his lap. A picture of them on their wedding day was his desktop picture, but he didn't call attention to the image. Instead, he opened a folder labeled 'The_-Fairy_Sept_SirenSF'.

He clicked open some pictures, and Maia saw herself. It was the night she went to Siren with her friend Tahlia. Calen opened a movie file, which showed his fairy amongst the crowd at Tahlia's table. It was grainy and short, no more than a minute, but once it was over, it restarted on a loop.

Maia twisted in his lap so she could see his face. "I don't understand. Why did you go back to find the security footage of me from back then?"

Calen stroked her hair and ran his hand down her back.

"I had Mike get this for me the day after you went to Siren the first time."

Maia made a face. "What? What do you mean?"

He tugged on a lock of her hair. "When I saw you at that warehouse, in the Russian's hands, I'd already been looking for you for weeks."

Her brow wrinkled. "You were *what*?"

Calen let out a frustrated breath. "I saw you that night. You passed by me in the hallway. It was dark and you didn't see me. But I saw you. It was crazy. Like those scenes in movies. Everything slowed down and you floated past me. It was only for a few seconds. I thought you weren't real," he said laughing a little. "In that light you were...unearthly. I followed you but lost you in the crowd in the next room. So I went to my office and located you on the security feeds, but when I went back down, you and your party were gone." He leaned back in the chair and tweaked her hair again.

"I looked for you in the nights after, too. Mike thought I was crazy. I would spend hours poring over security footage. Eventually, he realized I was looking for a specific girl. Imagine my shock when we saw you again."

Maia's mouth was open. Then she smiled and said, "No way. I don't believe you."

"Do you want to call Mike right now? He'll tell you."

Maia studied him in silence, her cute little face thoughtful. "If this is true, why didn't you mention it before? Like when you showed me your collection?"

Calen passed a hand over her waist and down her leg. He closed the computer and pushed it aside before picking up his wife and setting her on the desk in front of him.

"I didn't want you to think you were at the mercy of some psycho stalker," he said eventually, his hands running up and down her body freely now.

Maia glanced at his hands, which were undressing her now. When he went for her panties, she stopped him, looking at him earnestly.

"Do you think it was fate?" she whispered, her big, teal-colored eyes trained on him.

He shrugged. "I don't know. I don't care. I'm just glad I found you."

She put her hands on his, and she slowly guided him under her skirt. He worked her panties off in record time and she started to unbutton his shirt. But he was faster than she was. Before Maia was done with his shirt he had unfastened his pants and pushed them down with his boxers.

With hot hungry hands he hauled her to him, pulling her legs open roughly and stepping between them. He took a fistful of her hair and used it to tug her gently toward him before taking her lips in a hard kiss designed to scramble her senses. Instead, it served to sharpen his own hunger.

He reached between Maia's legs to stroke her until she was wet enough to take him. As soon as she was ready, he grabbed her hips and pulled her toward him. He plunged his cock into her a little roughly, and she cried out—but not in pain.

Pushed hard by his hunger, he stroked into her harder than he ever had before. She moaned in response, opening her legs a little wider to give him better access. The heat between them rose quickly, burning hotter and faster with each stroke.

Maia put her mouth against the hollow of his neck, kissing and sucking like mad. Feverishly, she tasted his sweat, not noticing that she was scratching him, marking his skin as they rocked together.

A few more thrusts, and Maia tightened like a bowstring around him, her nails digging in hard as she climaxed with a loud moan. She held him tight until eventually her body went lax around him.

He kissed her again, her hands passing over the little crescents she had made on his sides. Calen ignored the scratches as he gathered her closer, wrapping his hands around her hot little ass cheeks as he held her against him.

"Wrap your legs around me, nymph," he ordered.

Maia was weak, but she immediately complied. He lifted her clear off the desk, spinning around until her back met the bookcase behind them. She was so petite, it was easy to hold her against him as he ground into her, intentionally rocking their bodies against the prized volumes of his collection.

He lifted Maia, holding her helplessly against him as he worked her up and down his cock.

"*Calen,*" she whispered plaintively, her hand moving over his heart.

Did she believe in them now?

"You feel so good baby, so hot and soft," he murmured as he pinned her to the bookcase, fucking her hard and fast.

Maia responded by clenching her inner muscles tight around him.

"*Shit,*" he breathed, shoving against her as he worked a hand higher against her ass.

He probed her little rosette with his hand, teasing and pushing. She tensed against him, and he soothed her with an inarticulate sound as he pushed past the tight ring of muscle. The dual stimulation proved to be too much. Maia clamped down on him, holding his cock tightly.

"Come with me, Calen," she gasped.

It was more than enough to send him over the edge. He gripped her bottom hard, pumping into her twice more before his cock jerked and he exploded. His hot seed spilled inside her as she milked him through each excruciating pulse.

"Shit!" he swore as the last spasms racked his body.

With the last of his strength, he turned back around and deposited Maia lightly onto the desk's mahogany surface. Out of breath, she collapsed on it. He dropped down into his desk chair and pulled it closer to her.

He rested his head on Maia's stomach and reached out to cover her racing heart with his hand.

They stayed like that for a long time. He turned to look at her, pleased to see he wasn't the only one having trouble catching their breath. He ran his fingers up and down her chest, tracing her collarbone.

"I love you, Maia."

Maia sucked in a breath and tried to sit up, but he stopped her, holding her down with his hand.

"Are you sure?" she asked him worriedly.

He laughed. "Yes, I'm sure."

"I—" she began, but he cut her off by covering her mouth.

"No," he said decisively. "Not yet. Not till you're sure."

Maia made a muffled 'I'm sure' sound, but he shook his head.

"I need you to be certain. One hundred percent and then some," he said seriously.

If she said she loved him right now, it might be because he'd prompted her or she felt obligated to say it back.

Maia responded by biting him. He snatched his hand away, trying not to laugh. "I—I hope we made a baby," she said.

He stroked her hair and looked into her amazing blue-green eyes for a long time.

It might not have been 'I love you', but it was pretty damn close.

"Me too," he said, picking her up and carrying her to their bed.

CHAPTER 26

The weeks that followed were the happiest of Maia's life. Calen had told her he loved her, and she knew she loved him, too. She had been afraid to admit it to herself before, but his confession had broken down the protective walls inside her heart.

Those walls had been there a long time, ever since her mother had died. It wasn't only shyness that kept her from becoming close to others. She knew that now. Protecting herself from feeling that kind of loss again had become second nature. Her fear had held her back from making connections, friends, and more.

She wanted to tell Calen how she felt about him. It felt cowardly, keeping silent. The words were there, on the tip of her tongue, but every time she tried to get them out, she was swamped with uncertainty and panic.

I'll just have to wait for the perfect moment, she decided. The words would come easily then. And maybe, if she was lucky, she would be able to tell him she was pregnant at the same time. That possibility was looking more likely every day.

Her period was over a week late. Calen had been out of town to check on his west coast clubs, so he hadn't been around to notice. But she had always been regular before, and she was anxious to confirm her self-diagnosis. However, getting an appointment with her gynecologist before the Thanksgiving holiday proved impossible.

Maia contemplated going to the drugstore for a pregnancy test, but she couldn't do it in front of Davis and Stephens. They might report the trip to Calen. And she didn't want him to know yet. What if she was wrong?

How long would delivery take if she ordered one online? *Too long.* She needed to know before Calen came home tomorrow. The uncertainty was starting to drive her to distraction. Not to mention the fact Calen served wine with every meal. It would be suspicious if she suddenly started turning it down. He would definitely notice. And if this was a false alarm, she would have gotten his hopes up for nothing.

The lab was almost empty, so she couldn't ask a friend to go and get her a test. Not that there was one she would have trusted with something like that. Well, there was Tahlia, but she wasn't answering her texts again.

Maybe if I ask Davis very, very nicely he would run to the drugstore and get a test for me, Maia thought as she grabbed the samples she needed to prepare for the DNA sequencer. Davis would be discreet if she swore him to secrecy. She'd have to wait to get him alone because Stephens would squeal like a little girl.

Her husband was due back tomorrow, so if she was going ask, she had to do it now. Removing her latex gloves, she texted Davis and asked him to come into her office. Except for Wes and Chang, the lab's office was deserted. Everyone else had left early for the holiday.

When Davis came in, Maia made her request. She was blushing madly, but she didn't stammer. "Davis can you go to the drugstore for me? I need a pregnancy test. Please don't mention it to Calen. I could be wrong, and I don't want to get his hopes up."

The big man broke out into an even bigger grin. "Okay, but I'll need to move Stephens inside while I'm out getting the test. He can watch without getting in the way with only Wes here."

"Oh, did Chang leave? I wanted to say goodbye before he left."

"He's joining you for Thanksgiving dinner at the Caislean tomorrow," he reminded her.

"Yeah, but he wanted to find out what he should bring. I think the hotel's chef is preparing all the food, but he wanted bring chocolates or flowers. I was supposed to text Maggie to ask which would be preferable," Maia said, pursing her lips.

With all of the work she was doing, she'd forgotten.

"I'll have Stephens do that for you," Davis said, "You look busy," he added, looking at the many samples in front of her.

Maia nodded ruefully, slipping on her lab coat. "Thanks. I think I'm going to be here late enough as it is."

Once he was gone, she carried her samples to the little room that housed the DNA sequencer and got to work. She spent most of the next hour preparing and loading her samples, finishing a little later than she'd intended. It was dark outside as she made her way back to the lab with her leftover materials.

With any luck Davis had completed his errand and she could take a pregnancy test as soon as she arrived home.

MAIA STEPPED through the empty corridors, happy she was finally done. The DNA sequencer had been booked solid in the last week, but with everyone leaving for the holiday early, a timeslot had finally opened up, and she'd finally been able to process her samples.

She turned the corner, her sneakers silent on the tiles, and almost screamed her head off.

Lying in the middle of the hallway was an unconscious Stephens, blood all over his chest and stomach.

Maia turned and ran blindly back the way she came. In the distance, doors slammed, and she ducked around the corner, catching a glimpse of a large tattooed man as he ran out of a door down the hall. She couldn't be sure, but the ink on his arms resembled what she'd seen on the men in the woods. Cyrillic tattoos.

Shit, Shit, Shit.

Peeking around the corner, she saw the stranger hovering over Stephens. Edging away from the corner as quietly as possible, she ducked into a door that led to an empty lab. The professor it used to belong to hadn't gotten tenure, and the entire staff had moved to a lab in the Midwest. The space was currently being used for storage.

For a second, she contemplated locking both doors to the room, but the Russians could easily shoot through them if they suspected she was in there. The frosted glass windows in the doors were opaque, but they might still be able to make out her shadow. Putting down the rack of tubes she was holding in a death grip, she slipped out of her white lab coat and shoved it into an empty cabinet. Crouching low, she made her way to the far door.

Praying silently, Maia opened the door as quietly as she could. There was no one in sight. Holding her breath, she went for the basement door in a quick crawl. If she was lucky, there were only one or two assassins looking for her. There was a chance she could escape to the neighboring BioLabs building using the connecting tunnel.

She crept down the stairs, unsure if she could even hear the Russians over the pounding of her heart. When she reached the bottom of the stairs, she listened intently, but there were no sounds of pursuit. Staying in the dark, she headed for the connecting tunnel.

She had almost reached it when she heard a crashing noise in the distance ahead of her. Almost tripping, she dived for cover as another Russian, a tall thick one, came out of the BioLabs tunnel.

Oh god, please don't let them have started searching in the wrong building. If they had, there was no telling how many people they might have shot in the process. The BioLabs was a much bigger building, and there would have been a lot more people there, even the day before thanksgiving.

Crouching behind a liquid nitrogen tank, Maia held her breath as the man walked past her. He had reached the stairs when the door above opened. One of the Russians from the woods, the fat one Calen had told her was called Timur, called down from the top. His harsh words were completely unintelligible, but they sent a cold chill down her spine.

Tears ran down her cheeks as she started to shiver uncontrollably. Holding a hand to her mouth to stifle any sound, she cowered in the corner as the larger Russian replied to whatever Timur had said. Then he turned and walked back the way he had come. At the top of the stairs, Timur disappeared, shutting the door behind him.

Cautiously, Maia leaned forward, not wanting to lose sight of the larger man. He disappeared behind the door leading to the Bio Labs tunnel. She waited to see if he came back, but he didn't. For a long time, she crouched on the floor, hugging her knees. If she was right, the big Russian was waiting for her on the other side of the door, and Timur was upstairs searching for her with god knows who else.

Stephens might be dead. Maybe Wesley, too, if he hadn't gone home yet. He was local and might have ducked out to start his holiday early. At least she hoped he had. Where was Davis? The trip to the drugstore wouldn't have taken that long. He would have been monitoring the camera feeds from the van.

The cameras!

Oh god, where were they? She hadn't asked in case someone noticed her looking directly at one. If she didn't know where they were, she couldn't give away their location. The cameras had to have caught her coming down the stairs at least. Which means they saw the big intruder, too. If her luck hadn't completely run out, Davis had gotten back to the van unseen by the Russians and was calling the police now. She prayed they hadn't seen him before he saw them. But she had to consider the possibility that they had.

Maia had to find a better hiding place. She was too exposed. If the Russians backtracked, they might spot her. She stayed frozen in place for a few more breathless seconds, trying to psych herself up enough to move out of the dark corner. Eventually, she crept away, aiming for one of the adjoining storage rooms. It only had one entrance, but there were several cabinets. She might be able to squeeze into one.

Once inside, she realized there was only one solid option available for a hiding place...and for a split second, she thought letting the Russians find her might be a better alternative.

Swallowing hard, she moved deeper into the room.

CHAPTER 27

*C*alen was on his private plane halfway back home, pleased that he'd been able to wrap up his business at his west coast clubs early. It had almost killed him, but he'd pushed through every meeting quickly. He hated leaving Maia, even for just a few days.

Leaning back in his chair, he picked up one the boxes lying next to him. It was an extra special gift his wife was sure to love. Calen had started out giving her perfumes and jewelry. But the perfumes gave her a headache, so he'd stuck with jewelry for a while. She always thanked him sweetly, but she would also ask him not to spend so much money on her. Combined with the fact she never wore any of the accessories—indeed seemed to forget all about them—he'd decided to get creative when it came to gift-giving.

He had contacted one of his personal shoppers and had given him the task of tracking down displays of rare butterflies. His buyer, used to purchasing clothes and high-end alcohol, had been a little thrown by the task. But he'd risen to the occasion and found exactly what Calen was looking for in various antique collections.

Calen now had hundreds of museum-quality specimens mounted in special shadow box cases. He couldn't wait to give them to Maia.

His cell phone rang. Still picturing Maia's face when she opened her gift, he answered without noting the caller ID.

"Is this Calen McLachlan?" an unknown voice asked in Russian.

He sat up abruptly. "Who is this?"

"My name is Viktor. I met you when you acquired your wife," the stranger said, no trace of mockery in his voice.

"What's going on? Why are you calling me?" he asked in Russian, dread settling in his stomach like acid.

"The Komarov has given me leave to inform you of a problem. He does not want trouble."

"What the fuck is going on? Is it Timur?"

The stranger paused. "Yes. He has developed a...fixation. Since you cheated him of his prize, he has been indulging in more of his vices lately. The drugs are making him paranoid. More than usual. He will not listen to reason."

"Has he gone after her? Did he...take her?" he whispered, his throat threatening to close up on him.

It may have been his imagination, but he thought Viktor might have sounded sorry for him. "I'm not sure. But he's missing, and some of his less-intelligent followers are with him. One of his regular girls said he wouldn't stop ranting about you and your wife before he took off today."

"If he touches one fucking hair on her head, I will kill him! I will kill him if he's gotten anywhere near her! Do you understand?" he hissed, resisting the impulse to smash the phone into pieces.

There was a pointed silence. "It may be too late. The Komarov is prepared to make reparations should that be the case."

"No fucking way! Tell the Komarov I will make sure he and the rest of your fucking crew burn if he doesn't call off his waste of a son!"

"I told him you would say as much," Viktor said in a resigned tone. "I will attempt to recover Timur, but I'm still far out from the school."

It was only then that Calen recognized the traffic noises in the background, horns blaring as Viktor sped through the streets.

"Fuck!"

He hung up without another word. For a split second, he was frozen with indecision. Then he dialed the one man he knew could mobilize an army on short notice.

He answered on the second ring.

"Jason! I need your help."

MAIA SQUEEZED HER EYES SHUT, trying hard to keep her mouth, eyes, and nose out of the stinking liquid surrounding her. She took several deep calming breaths out of her mouth. If she tried to breathe through her nose, the smell would overpower her. And she needed to make sure she stayed absolutely silent.

Her hand brushed against something next to her, and she suppressed a shudder as she pictured the dead things floating around her.

I hate fish, she thought as some of them pressed against her body. She was never going to eat sushi again.

Maia had hidden in the only thing capable of hiding her in the storage space, the ichthyologist's storage trunk. Surrounded by a blue liquid that smelled of metal and oil, were preserved fish—specimens unique enough to be kept on hand for further study. She hadn't been entirely sure that she would fit, but luck was with her. The trunk was only half-full.

She craned her ear up out of the liquid, but when she did the side of her face was submerged instead. Straightening her head, her ear dropped below the surface of the liquid again. The sounds she was straining to hear would be muffled, but she couldn't risk the liquid getting into her eyes and mouth. She had no idea what it was.

Oh God.

What if she actually was pregnant? What was she floating in? She could be submerged in a toxic bath of mutagens, her baby inside her. For a mad moment, she fought the urge to bolt from her hiding place, her desperation to get rid of the muck she was covered in strong and sharp.

With effort, she forced herself to stay in her hiding place, knowing that she could be running straight into the Russian's arms if she moved.

Trying to calm herself, Maia pictured Calen, his beautiful face and strong, tall body. What she wouldn't give to be in his arms again. Desperate and afraid, she relived every moment spent with him, every touch and look.

She should have told him she loved him. Waiting for the perfect time had been a poor excuse. She'd been a coward, afraid to trust his feelings for her, that he would realize telling her he loved her was a mistake and take it back. If she ever saw him again, she would tell him everything.

For now, she could only wait and hope rescue was coming.

CHAPTER 28

$\mathcal{B}$y the time his private jet landed at the airport, Calen was frantic. He made terrified phone calls to everyone he knew. In his desperation, he even called his father and cousin. No one had any information for him. Trick and Liam were rushing to the campus now. The police and the FBI were already at the school, tearing the place apart, but there was no sign of Maia or the Russians.

A worried Jason called him to say they had found Stephens and Davis hurt inside. Stephens was in critical condition from a gunshot wound to the chest. Davis had called the police before going inside to find Stephens when he had seen the Russians in the building. He'd taken a bullet too, but Jason had said it wasn't critical.

Please let her be all right. Please.

Time seemed to slow as he was driven to the university's campus. Liam and Trick were texting him updates. They had gotten there first but hadn't been allowed in the building.

Eventually, his car pulled up to Divinity Avenue, the street where Maia's building was located. His driver got as close as he could, but they were stopped by a wall of police cars. He jumped out and ran, only to be stopped by uniformed officers.

"My wife—is my wife okay? Is Maia okay?" he shouted.

MAIA WAITED FOR AN ETERNITY, silent tears slipping into the blue liquid around her. She couldn't understand what was taking so long. Shouldn't the police be here by now? Or Davis was dead, and no help was coming.

She almost jumped up when she heard muffled bangs and shouts start in the distance. Was it the cavalry? Or had the Russians finally found her? Did they have reinforcements?

Maia focused on trying to make out the words, but the liquid muffled her hearing. Cringing, she turned, her eyes shut tight as she submerged her right side again so she could get her ear above the liquid's surface.

"Maia McLachlan, are you there?" an unknown voice called. "This is special agent Ethan Thomas."

Her breath came out in a rush. She stifled the impulse to run out of her hiding place. What if it was a trick? More footsteps pounded down the stairs.

"Maia! It's Jason. If you're there, answer me!"

"Jason! I'm here! I'm here!" Maia shouted as she pushed the loose lid of the crate back, scrambling up gingerly.

She had probably damaged some of the specimens, but she didn't care. Blue liquid streamed from her as she ran toward the voices.

CALEN WAS STRUGGLING against the cops holding him back from Maia's building when a figure broke away from a cluster of people farther down the street. It was Liam running toward him.

"It's okay. They found her. She's okay!"

"Oh, thank god," he said, bending over knees suddenly too weak to support him.

Liam threw an arm around him and hauled him up.

Trick rushed to their side. "They said we can't go in, but they're going to bring her out soon."

"Is she hurt?" he asked, his stomach painful as he leaned on Liam for support.

"No, I don't think so," Trick said as they settled down to wait.

Time slowed to a painful crawl. Calen paced with barely contained impatience outside of the building. Maia had been found, but they didn't know her condition other than she was walking around. Behind him Trick, his father, and Darren were waiting with concerned expressions. Even Darren tried to comfort him.

"She's all right, they already said," his cousin said, patting him awkwardly on the back.

"Then why isn't she out here? They would have brought her out here if she was all right!"

No one answered, and he resumed pacing, wondering where the hell Liam had got to.

Finally, after what seemed like an endless number of minutes, a shout went up at the front of the buildings. Liam was standing with Jason and his partner Ethan. For some reason, the latter was naked from the waist up. Jason moved aside slightly, talking to someone. And then he saw her, walking toward him on her own steam.

Calen almost collapsed again in relief. He rushed toward her and Maia looked relieved, up until the moment he put his hands on her. "No, no! Don't touch me! I don't know what it is," she said, warding him off with her palms out.

Too relieved to heed her words, he hugged her tight, squeezing hard enough to make her squeal. Tears stung his eyes, and he fought not to cry in front of half the city.

"Are you okay?" he asked softly

"I'm fine. How is Stephens?" she asked anxiously from the circle of his arms, her little brow wrinkled with concern.

"I don't know baby. He's still in surgery."

At least that's what he thought Trick had told him.

"Oh, god! Calen, it's all over you!" Maia exclaimed, pushing him away.

Confused, he looked down. His wife was wearing was a man's button down shirt, a white one, except for the parts that were stained with something blue. She was still wearing her jeans, which were also stained dark with the sticky liquid. Now he knew why Ethan was half naked.

Maia broke away suddenly.

"Baby what's wrong?" he called after her.

She had reached one of the ambulances parked out front and was talking fast, gesturing wildly to the EMTs. They scrambled to attention, and one came toward him, a bucket of something in his hand.

"Sir, we're going to need your clothes."

CHAPTER 29

*M*aia had been so paranoid about whatever it was they were covered with, she stripped out of her jeans in the street and consequently wore nothing but Ethan's shirt under Liam's coat for the car ride home. She shivered in his arms the whole way.

Now Calen and the men were waiting for Maia in the living room. They had both taken showers as soon as they arrived home, despite the fact the EMTs had doused both of them with ice-cold water in the middle of the street.

But one shower wasn't enough for Maia. She had finished the first and had joined them in the living room for two minutes, before turning around and announcing she needed another one.

"Did you find out what that stuff was?" Trick asked when Calen stopped to pour himself another drink.

He shook his head. "Her boss is looking into it."

Now that the adrenaline was wearing off, his head was starting to pound. What the hell were his father and Darren doing? They had taken him aside and told him not to worry about Timur. Their assurances that the Russians would never get near Maia again should have troubled him, but he didn't care. He knew that right then his father was demanding Timur's head on a platter, and it didn't bother him at all.

Calen snorted. He might be his father's son after all.

The FBI agents on campus had been watching Colman and Darren with barely concealed shock and interest. They probably couldn't believe their eyes. His father was notoriously private and didn't allow himself to be photographed often. But there he was, out in the open, surrounded by hundreds of members of law enforcement.

However, since his father wasn't currently wanted for any questioning, all those cops had been forced to stand back and let him leave when it was all over. It was a safe bet that they were all watching Colman and Darren closely right now in the hopes he would make some sort of mistake they could finally pin on him.

"It was pretty smart of her to climb into that fish tank. If the preservative wasn't toxic, that is," Liam said, sipping his own scotch.

"I'm sure it isn't," he mumbled. "They wouldn't keep that stuff around if it was poisonous."

"I don't know, man," Trick chimed in. "Peyton says they keep lots of toxic chemicals in labs like Maia's."

"When did you see Peyton?" Calen asked.

"Didn't you see her?"

He sighed. "No."

"Both she and Maggie were there, man," Trick said.

"I'm surprised you didn't notice her ogling Ethan's bare chest," Liam growled.

Calen wrinkled his nose. "Maggie was checking out another man? In front of Jason?"

"No. *Peyton* was," Liam said, sounding unaccountably frustrated.

Calen thought that was weird, but he forgot about it the moment Maia walked back into the living room. She was wearing yoga pants and some thick wool socks. She was also wearing one of his sweaters —had probably pulled it on for extra comfort. But her hair was still wet, and he was glad he'd asked Trick to start a fire.

"Has Dr. Schroeder called back yet?" Maia asked anxiously as Calen wrapped her in a hug.

"Not yet, nymph. He's making some calls. As soon as he finds out what the blue stuff is, he's going to call back. He's glad you're not hurt, by the way," he said, pulling her down onto the couch and into his lap.

He stroked her wet hair and held her tightly. He didn't ever plan on letting go.

"Are you sure you're okay, honey?" Liam asked.

Calen and Trick gave each other a speaking glance. Liam's tone was uncharacteristically soft and soothing. His best friend was a gruff bastard most of the time. Liam didn't make the effort to soften to his bull in a china shop approach unless he really liked someone, and often not even then.

But Maia had clearly been through a lot. Her bodyguards had been shot, and she had been hunted, and forced to hide in a pool of dead fish to save her own life.

"I managed to hide before anyone saw me. I'm just worried about Stephens now. And Wesley. Did anyone track him down? Did he get out in time?"

"Yeah, the kid went home early," Calen answered. "Baby, why did Davis miss the Russians entering the building? He told Jason that when he got back they were already inside. Why did he leave his post?"

Maia looked nervous. "He was running an errand for me."

"*Maia!* The bodyguards aren't your servants," Calen scolded. "They are there to protect you. Not pick up your dry cleaning."

"He wasn't picking up my dry cleaning. And he left Stephens inside with me for extra security. Stephens was waiting in my office while I ran some samples on a machine on the other side of the building. Look, I have to call Dr. Schroeder, okay?"

She struggled out of his lap and went to the phone.

Soon they could hear her in the distance, asking her boss's wife if he could call her back as soon as possible. The anxiety in her voice was clear. Calen frowned when she finally returned.

"Baby, I'm sure the blue stuff was fine," Calen said. "Those fish biologists have to dig around those tanks all the time, so I'm sure it's safe."

Maia paced, cordless phone in hand. She shook her head. "I'm not sure anyone has used those specimens in years."

Calen sat back. Maia was totally twisted in knots about the wrong thing. She had barely mentioned the Russians at all since they got home.

"You think you're pregnant, don't you?" Liam asked out of the blue.

Calen turned to stare at him, but Liam was watching Maia. He swiveled to her and did a double take. He had expected an immediate denial, but she was silent, and her face was stricken.

"Baby?"

"I—I'm not sure," she said finally.

Calen froze, blood rushing to his ears, filling them with static. It lasted a few seconds until a warm feeling of intense relief flooded him. Rushing to his wife, he swept her off her feet. He felt like throwing her up in the air and catching her like an infant, but he shut that impulse down and settled for swinging her around instead.

Maia squealed. "Put me down. If I'm pregnant this can't be good."

Calen relented and set her on her feet.

"Calen, the blue stuff," she began.

He nodded, finally understanding the source of her anxiety. "I'll make some calls," he promised, but he still wasn't worried about the blue liquid. Well, not as worried as his wife...

"Did Davis leave a bag for me?" she asked.

"Yeah, over here," Trick called, holding a brown paper bag.

Maia walked over and snatched it up, holding it to her chest. She gave Calen a meaningful look and disappeared into the hallway. He followed her, and she opened the bag. It was an assortment of different pregnancy tests.

Davis had taken his mission seriously. And he had apparently been confused about what kind to buy, so he'd bought the entire pregnancy test selection. Probably from more than one store, by the looks of it. Calen understood why Davis left his post now, but he was still going to read him the riot act when he was finally out the hospital.

"Okay, baby, go take one of these, or five, and get back out here. I'll track down whoever put those fish in that tank."

Maia let out a breath and nodded. She retreated to their bedroom, and he went back out to the guys.

"Trick is calling for you. He's got the head of the Harvard chemistry department on the phone," Liam said when he returned. "And Jason is on his way up. He's spitting nails about being kept in the dark. He wants to know why a Russian crew wants your wife dead."

Calen nodded, no longer tired. Maia was safe, and she might be pregnant. Nothing else was going to get to him. He might never let her out of his sight again, but he was otherwise unfazed.

A few minutes later, Jason arrived with his partner Ethan. Ethan had found a t-shirt somewhere, but it looked like it was a size too small. Liam snorted and gave him a dismissive once over.

Weird. He'd always thought Liam liked Jason's partner.

"What the hell is going on?" Jason demanded.

Calen looked at Liam and gestured to Ethan with a small nod. His friend understood, but he didn't look happy about it. "Ethan, why don't you have a drink, over here? Way over here," Liam said, walking out of the room and heading to the library.

Ethan shot his partner a look that said he wasn't going anywhere, but Jason shook his head wearily. Rolling his eyes, Ethan followed Liam, his entire stance radiating his reluctance.

"Sit down, Jason," Calen said. "Let me tell you how I met my wife."

CHAPTER 30

The explanation took the better part of a half hour, mostly because Jason kept interrupting. The agent couldn't believe they hadn't told him about the possible danger to Maia, and by extension Maggie and Peyton.

"They were never in any danger when they were with her," Calen assured him. "There were always two or more bodyguards with them at all times."

"Fat lot of good that did tonight," Jason argued. "Both of your guards got shot and god knows what statutes you broke going to meet the Russians in the first place."

"None. None that will stick anyway. Liam checked with his lawyer, and I did my own due diligence. The Russians were offering restitution willingly, and I was merely negotiating a final sum."

"And failing to report an assault, kidnapping, and a murder!"

Calen ran his hands through his hair. "Jason, you can't tell Ethan about that. Not about what Maia saw. They will have moved the body by now anyway," he said, folding his hands in front of him. "And I won't let her testify. They would never stop hunting her down if she did."

Jason argued with him, but Calen was adamant. "It's the only way to keep her safe!" he hissed. "This is the love of my life we are talking about. If it was Maggie, you would do the same thing!"

Jason closed his eyes and rubbed his hand over them, and Calen knew he had won.

"All right," Jason growled. "I'll tell Ethan enough to satisfy him and try to keep the rest of the department off your back for as long as I can. But it won't be for long. They'll want answers."

"That's why I have an entire team of lawyers," Calen answered as he noticed Maia peeking at them from around the corner.

Fuck! The test! He'd completely forgotten.

"Baby? Come here," he ordered, gesturing to her. She looked uncertainly at Jason, but she walked over to him and he scooped her up in his arms. "Well?"

She nodded and he let out a whoop as he hugged her close.

"What is it?" Ethan asked, hurrying back with Liam when they heard his shout.

"You can be the first to congratulate us," Calen said, his protective arms encircling Maia's waist. "We're pregnant."

THEY DIDN'T GO to bed for hours that night. Dr. Schroeder finally called to inform them that the blue liquid was harmless. It was a mixture of preservatives, alcohol, and buffering agents. The blue color was simple food dye.

It wasn't great that Maia was lying in it for so long, but he'd been assured by the head of the chemistry department that nothing in the solution would affect her or their baby, particularly since she'd made sure she didn't get any in her eyes, nose, or mouth.

Ethan was hard to shake in the end. When Colman called, the big FBI agent tried to follow him into the library, but Maia herself pulled him away and back to the living room.

By the time Calen was done talking to his father, she had the former army ranger wrapped around her little finger. She didn't tell

Ethan why the Russians were after her, but she'd described what happened in the building. In great detail.

Ethan pressed her for more, but Calen threatened to call his lawyers, plural. So Ethan finally left with Jason, still looking pissed.

"What did your father say?" Trick asked after the two men were gone.

Liam looked at him expectantly, but Calen shook his head and told them to go home. They'd been frustrated, but the look on his face was enough to make them leave. It was better that they never know what his father had told him. Maia, too, for that matter. All she needed to know was that Timur would never bother her again.

Calen had gone to sleep holding his wife tight in his arms. But this time she didn't complain about his grip. Instead she burrowed harder against his chest, like she was trying to crawl inside him.

CHAPTER 31

The next few days were hard on his wife. Maia was extremely jumpy and could barely sleep. Calen did everything he could, including getting a trauma counselor to come and talk to her, but she was too distracted by the aftermath of her ordeal to enjoy Thanksgiving.

They had decided to cancel on the Tyler brothers in favor of staying home alone, but Liam wouldn't hear of that, and the whole party had shifted to Calen's penthouse instead. Maia had politely gone through the motions, but it was obvious her mind was elsewhere. He could tell she was still anxious. Everyone else probably could, too, but they were too polite to say anything.

Chang had made some excited enquiries at first, but Peyton had taken him aside and had spoken to him quietly. He calmed down and stopped trying to press Maia for details. Calen had given Peyton a grateful look, reminding himself to do something nice for her soon. She was turning into a good friend for Maia. So was Maggie, for that matter.

The only person missing had been Maia's friend Tahlia. They hadn't been able to reach her so it was assumed she had gone home to Florida for the holiday.

After dinner, Jason took him aside. "Look, I stonewalled my superiors as much as possible. They are none too happy with the wall of bullshit your lawyers have thrown up. But it's not going to blow over until Maia makes a statement."

"They can have one in writing. Liam and I already put our heads together about what it should say," he said, keeping one eye on Maia and Peyton as they chatted on the couch while he and Jason wandered over to the bar.

Across the room, Maia gave Peyton a quick smile. She hadn't smiled at all since the attack. His shoulders eased, a tight little coil of anxiety loosening inside him. His fairy was going to be all right.

I definitely need to buy Peyton something nice. Maybe a car.

"Well, what is it?" Jason asked, after accepting a glass of whiskey.

Calen turned back to him and waved him into his office. They sat in the leather armchairs by the fireplace and leaned closer to each other.

"Maia will sign something that says she witnessed Timur Komarov —and Timur alone—taking drugs in the woods and burying a bag. She did not see what was inside but assumed it was more drugs since Timur had taken her hostage afterwards. The rest we'll tell the truth about, more or less."

Jason took a bracing sip from his glass, but he nodded. Calen didn't bother to add that his father had already run their official story past the Komarov. The Komarov had approved, but Timur's ultimate fate was still undecided.

A few days passed quietly before they heard anything. Then Darren stopped by to quietly inform him that Timur wasn't going to be a problem anymore. They didn't know much, but Colman had been assured that they would never see Timur again.

Calen knew it was too much to hope that Timur was dead when he heard that. If he was dead, a body would have been produced as a show of good faith. The best he could hope for was that Timur had been banished. Darren implied the Komarov had gotten sick of his son's shit and was no longer offering him protection. Timur had either run on his own or had been sent back to Russia.

207

He tried to console himself with the fact Timur might be freezing his balls off in Siberia, but he would have preferred the little shit had ended up floating in the Charles.

Surprisingly, Darren had demanded to be the one to explain the situation to Maia. Calen hadn't wanted to let him, explaining that Maia was a little fragile right now, but Darren bulldozed through the penthouse calling for her before he could stop him. However, in the end, his cousin had been the picture of comfort and chivalrous concern.

Calen had scowled when Darren had wrapped an arm around Maia while he sat next to her on the couch. Stroking her comfortingly, he detailed the Russian's assurances and apologies. Calen was tempted to chop Darren's hands off, a sentiment that did not escape his cousin's attention.

The smirk Darren had given him over Maia's bright head was enough to tell him things were still basically normal between the two of them. But at least he was being nice to Maia. Darren had even hugged her as he said goodbye...although that may have only been to piss him off.

After Darren left, Calen found Maia in front of the Christmas tree he'd had delivered earlier that day, her arms wrapped tightly around herself. The tree wasn't decorated. He wanted to do that with Maia. She had mentioned she hadn't had one since her mother had passed.

"So he's not dead?" Maia asked, staring out the window.

He hugged her close. "Probably not, but he's cut off. Da has let it be known that if the little shit comes back to these parts, it will mean war." That was clearly the wrong thing to say. Maia's face turned ashen pale. "It won't come to that. I promise. The Russians won't bother for a waste of skin like Timur."

He decided to distract her. "Maia, baby, I think you should take your boss up on his offer to take some time off. You've been through a lot, and it's only a few more weeks till Christmas anyway."

Maia pursed her lips but nodded, eyes distant. She was exhausted after waking up several times a night with nightmares.

"Time off might be a nice way of saying don't come back," she said eventually. "I wouldn't be surprised if they asked me to leave the program, for everyone's safety."

"That won't be an issue," he promised. "Lots of high-profile people go to that school. Security concerns aren't new there."

"Yeah, but most of those students aren't living with a contract out on their life."

"Neither are you. Not anymore. If Timur is still alive, he won't be coming back here. He'd be signing his own death warrant," he assured her.

Maia didn't respond.

"Hey," he said, his hand under her chin to turn her toward him. "I'm not going to let anyone hurt you. Not ever."

And he meant every word. Even now, his contacts were hard at work, looking for Timur in Russia and other holes a piece of shit like him could hide in Europe. He hadn't imagined he would ever behave like his father's son, but when he looked at Maia's pale worried face, he didn't care anymore. He would do whatever he had to do to keep her and their baby safe.

Ironically, Liam and Trick were one hundred percent behind him. They were helping him with his search, which unfortunately hadn't turned up anything yet. But they weren't giving up, and neither was he.

Eventually, Maia nodded and looked at the tree. "It smells wonderful," she said absently.

He had an idea. "Why don't we decorate it tonight?" he asked. "I don't have any decorations yet, but we could go to the store and buy some."

The people he hired every Christmas had always decorated the tree, since he was usually busy, but he wanted to start all new traditions now that he had a family.

"You want to go out to a store?" Maia asked, her little brow creased. "You never go shopping. What happened to 'I have people for that'? Your personal shoppers even buy my underwear."

Calen laughed. "I think a little retail therapy would do us both good. Plus I think we should choose our Christmas ornaments ourselves. Let me call Davis and Reynolds," he said as he stood, pulling her up after him.

Picking up on his enthusiasm, Maia's expression brightened before she went to get dressed.

Davis had come back to work a few days after being shot. He'd insisted, even though he had an arm in a sling. And Calen had let him, although he told him in no uncertain terms that he was never to leave his post for any reason ever again. Maia could order any future pregnancy tests online.

Davis had nodded after apologizing repeatedly. He even offered to resign, but Calen knew this failure would only make him guard Maia even better. Plus Davis *had* left Stephens in her office. The other former army ranger had been outnumbered and had taken a bullet high in his stomach. But he had given as good as he got, shooting two of the Russians before he'd gone down. No bodies had been found, but there had been blood trails leading out the back entrance of the building.

Stephens was going to make a full recovery. In the meantime, Calen had temporarily replaced him. But he, too, would also be coming back to work once he was healed.

CHAPTER 32

*C*alen's instinct was spot on. Retail therapy did wonders. He and Maia had come back laden with packages. Reynolds had to go back and make several trips to the car before he could get all of their purchases upstairs to the penthouse.

Maia had even gone off with Reynolds and Davis on her own to choose a gift for him. He'd hated letting her out of his sight, but the mischievous smile on her face when they came back was enough to placate him. She wouldn't give him any hints about what she'd bought him, but she was adorably smug about it. He decided taking his wife shopping would become a regular pastime.

They also went to a specialty ornament store to pick out their holiday decorations. He and Maia had a lot of fun choosing lights and a set of matching ornaments as well as some specific novelty ones.

When he found a fairy princess with orange gold hair with elaborate butterfly wings in mid-flight, Calen bought two, resolving to keep one at his office at work and one for the tree. The tiny figure was blowing a kiss. Maia had chosen a baby's first Christmas ornament with starry eyes, and he had gotten choked up watching her.

They had also bought stockings and different decorations for the coffee table and their library. He had asked Maia to share the library with him so they could work in the same space if they felt like it. He would move her desk in there eventually, but there wasn't a big hurry since they didn't keep the same work hours. But sharing his private domain made him feel closer to her, and Maia loved being surrounded by all the books.

Calen especially liked having her possessions around him while he worked late at night. He'd even had a special case installed to display Maia's butterfly collection next to his shelf of first editions, but for now it stood empty until she opened her gifts on Christmas day.

That night, he and Maia stayed up late decorating their Christmas tree. They strung lights and hung the beautiful handcrafted ornaments. Maia had vetoed tinsel, preferring to see as many of the rich green needles under the decorations as possible.

Calen snapped a lot of pictures of Maia hanging ornaments and decorating. He even used the timer so he could get into some of the shots, like the one where he lifted her to his shoulders so she could hang the star at the top of the tree. He wanted to document as much of their first Christmas together as possible.

When they were done, Maia made hot apple cider with whipped cream. They sat with their mugs in front of the tree, admiring the effect of the lights and shiny ornaments while the fireplace crackled with a warm fire behind them.

"It looks beautiful. I love how everything smells with the tree. Can we sleep here?" she asked, cuddling closer.

"I'm glad you like it, but wouldn't our bed be more comfortable?" he joked before growing serious.

Maia must have noticed the change in his expression. "What's wrong?"

Calen didn't want to ask her what he'd been wondering. He was pretty sure he already knew the answer, but he needed to hear it out loud. Sighing, he tried not to consider that a weakness. For her, he would be weak.

"Maia, do you love me?" he asked, chest tight.

He didn't realize he was holding his breath until Maia's eyes got huge and she clapped a hand over her mouth. "Oh shit!" she exclaimed.

Calen frowned. "Definitely not the answer I was hoping for," he said flatly. To his surprise, she laughed. "Okay, now I'm kind of insulted."

"No, no! I just realized what an idiot I've been. I was waiting for the right time. I decided I would tell you once I was sure I was pregnant. But I hadn't confirmed it, and then I was in that storage tank with all those dead fish telling myself how stupid waiting had been. And afterwards..."

Calen nodded. "After you got distracted by the fact you thought you were poisoned. You were worried about the baby and...you are still worried because there were no arrests made after what happened."

"Yeah, I guess. I would have felt better if we'd gotten more than promises from the Russians."

"Like what?"

"Like Timur's head on a platter," she said in a low voice, not meeting his eyes.

Calen snorted softly. He'd been worried she wouldn't understand what he had to do if he ever found Timur. Well, she probably still wouldn't if his plans ever came to fruition, but for now, he was glad for the bloodthirsty streak in his tiny wife. Even if she didn't mean it.

Maia took a deep breath. "This is a god-awful time for this given what I just said...but I love you. I love you with all my heart. You are the most important thing in my life. And I'm glad that you are. I know this is going to sound weird given all that's happened and how scary it's been, but if all of that is what I had to go through to meet you and become your wife, then I'm not sorry it happened."

Calen dropped his head until his forehead touched hers. "I'm glad I found you, too. But trust me when I say, we didn't need the Russian's help. I was looking for you. I *would* have found you."

Maia clung to him and pressed her lips to his. Her sweet kisses became heated quickly, and Calen tried to drag her to the bedroom, but she didn't want to move.

They ended up making love under their Christmas tree. Maia fell asleep gazing up at the lights from his arms. Afterward, he carried her to their bedroom, feeling more relaxed than he had in a long time. He didn't realize until much later that it was because he'd finally heard the words he'd been waiting for.

CHAPTER 33

Christmas Eve was a beautiful day in Boston. It had snowed the night before, and everything was coated with a pristine layer of snow. Maia thought it was a pity that cars were going to be driving over it, turning it brown and sludgy. But for the moment, it was still beautiful. She gazed at the snow-dusted city from the tall floor-to-ceiling windows in Calen's penthouse until she heard him come in behind her.

"How did I know I would find you by the tree? Are you going to want one year round?" he asked, taking off his long cashmere coat.

Maia paused and actually thought about it. "Hmm. No. I don't think so. It would make it less special if we did. But don't think I'm not tempted. I was actually thinking how beautiful the snow is this winter."

"Was it not beautiful last winter?" he asked with a grin.

"In the abstract, it probably was, but I did not look forward to it. My apartment was always freezing at this time of the year. I think this winter has been the best I've ever spent in this town," she said.

Calen scowled briefly. "I remember the issues with your apartment. That reminds me. You should wear your new coat and change into your boots for tonight," he murmured, examining the light low heels she was wearing with her red wool dress. "Can't be too warm."

Maia smiled and reached up to adjust his crooked tie. She was getting used to having Calen fuss over her, but now that her pregnancy was confirmed by a doctor, he'd gone into overdrive. His concern felt good, so she humored him. Most of the time...

"All right, but only because the boots are more comfortable. In the future, I think I should get to pick my own outfit. What do you say to that?" she asked brushing imaginary lint off his shoulders.

Calen pursed his lips and eventually inclined his head. "All right, I'm going to give you that one. But you should go change now or we're going to be late."

"Are the gifts all packed?" she asked over her shoulder as they went to their room to grab her boots.

"Yes, all but one," he said.

"What one is that?" she asked digging around her closet.

Calen leaned against the bed. "I've decided to tell Liam and Trick I will open a place in the Caislean after all."

Maia's orange-gold head popped out the closet. "What? I thought you weren't going to open any more clubs. That the challenge was gone."

"Well, I've decided to take your advice," he said as she sat on the bed to pull on her boots.

"My advice? What advice was that?"

He watched her with a warm expression her as she tugged on the tall leather boots. "I've decided to open a bar instead. But a special one. One modeled on a speakeasy."

Maia stopped fastening her boot mid-zip. Her eyes lit up, and she sprang into his arms. "That is so brilliant! A real speakeasy?"

"With a secret entrance and everything. And after that, maybe a restaurant. More of a challenge. I decided we shouldn't limit ourselves anymore," he said.

"*We?*" she beamed, wrapping her arms around his neck.

"Well, you are my inspiration. I plan on stealing your ideas for the rest of our lives," he said, mirroring her bright, warm smile.

Maia laughed. "That sounds good to me."

The End

Continue the Singular Obsession Series with Sergei's story Stolen Angel, a Readers' Favorite Five Star Read!

Rabia Tanveer for Readers' Favorite wrote:
"Sergei and Ada's story is very compelling and the reader is breathless to read the end of their story. Of course, the reader is breathless because of their passion as well. Their chemistry is super hot…"

Thank you for reading Calen's Captive! Reviews are an author's bread and butter. If you liked the story please consider leaving one.

Subscribe to the Lucy Leroux Newsletter for a *free* novella!
www.authorlucyleroux.com/newsletter

or keep up with her L.B. Gilbert releases
www.elementalauthor.com/newsletter

ABOUT THE AUTHOR

Lucy Leroux is another name for USA Today Bestselling Author L.B. Gilbert.

Seven years ago Lucy moved to France for a one-year research contract. Six months later she was living with a handsome Frenchman and is now married with an adorable half-french daughter.

When her last contract ended Lucy turned to writing. Frustrated by the lack of quality romance erotica she created her own.

Cursed is the first of many regency novels. Additionally, she writes a bestselling contemporary series. The 'Singular Obsession' books are a combination of steamy romance and suspense that feature intertwining characters in their own stand-alone stories. Follow her on twitter or facebook, or check our her website for more news!

www.authorlucyleroux.com

facebook.com/lucythenovelist
twitter.com/lucythenovelist
instagram.com/lucythenovelist